The Brother

Rein Raud

The Brother

Translated from the Estonian
by Adam Cullen

OPEN LETTER
LITERARY TRANSLATIONS FROM THE UNIVERSITY OF ROCHESTER

Copyright © 2008 by Rein Raud
Translation copyright © 2016 by Adam Cullen
Originally published in Estonia as *Vend*

First edition, 2016
All rights reserved

Images by Asko Künnap. Used with permission. www.kynnap.ee/asko.

Library of Congress Cataloging-in-Publication Data: Available.
ISBN-13: 978-1-940953-44-1 / ISBN-10: 1-940953-44-8

*Adam Cullen's translation is supported in part by an award from
the Cultural Endowment of Estonia's Traducta grant programme.*

*This project is supported in part by an award from
the National Endowment for the Arts.*

ART WORKS.
arts.gov

Printed on acid-free paper in the United States of America.

Text set in Janson, an old-style serif typeface named for Dutch punch-cutter
and printer Anton Janson (1620–1687).

Design by N. J. Furl

Open Letter is the University of Rochester's nonprofit, literary translation press:
Lattimore Hall 411, Box 270082, Rochester, NY 14627

www.openletterbooks.org

The Brother

The day that had begun bright with sunshine darkened abruptly into black clouds in the afternoon, and the couple booms of thunder were followed by a downpour so heavy that not a single window was left open in the small town. Nothing and no one occupied the main square apart from a taxi, the driver of which was also already about to lose hope, when he saw approaching from the opposite side of the square a tall man dressed in a wide-brimmed hat, a drenched overcoat, and knee-high boots—and who was strolling toward him through the storm with an unflinching tranquility, as if he paid no heed to the dreadful weather.

He'll get the car wet, the taxi-driver thought, *but at least I won't have been waiting here for nothing.*

The man indeed stopped next to the taxi and opened the door.

"Are you free?" he asked.

"Yes, I am," the taxi-driver replied.

"Then that makes two of us," the man said, slammed the door shut, and strolled onward through the rain and into the howling darkness.

People differ. There are those who do harm to others, and those to whom harm is done; some of the latter are the kind it would seem fair to attack because they have enough strength for retaliation, and then there are others, who in their vileness outright provoke confrontation, as the harm done to them is nothing more than revenge that restores the great balance.

Laila was none of these, for although she attracted injustice like bees to heather, all who did her wrong were nevertheless secretly embarrassed. The lawyer, whom she had asked to handle the inheritance affairs after her mother's death, had looked away as he placed paper after paper of complicated legal wording on the desk for Laila to sign, and the notary, who read the long and incoherent documentation aloud to her, occasionally felt a lump rise to his throat when he thought about what would become of that pale young woman following the successful execution of the transaction. Even the bailiff, who came to evict Laila from the Villa and record her assets, spoke more politely with her than with anyone else, and unprecedentedly, both the moving truck and the movers, who removed their hats when they greeted Laila, were provided at the company's expense. Her current landlord was no different either—he frequently cursed himself for asking that kind of rent for the tiny attic-room with a ceiling that leaked a little in one corner (with the extra obligation of Laila doing his family's laundry for free); and even the goateed antiquarian, at whose shop Laila had finally gotten a job, constantly caught himself thinking that he was paying her shamelessly little, which of course caused him to ruminate on human nature and shake his head, but resulted in nothing else. Or else he would eat an éclair with his afternoon coffee, which was, in reality, bad for his health.

Laila herself had grown accustomed to her bad luck, just as children who manage to comprehend the world will grow accustom to their own mortality, and in truth, she didn't even particularly hope that anything might ever be different.

Until the knock at the door.

"I would have expected anything," Brother said while unlacing his knee-high boots; the brother, of whose existence she hadn't the slightest clue just a moment earlier, but whom—she now knew—she had awaited for so long.

"I would have expected anything, but not that," said Brother. "When I arrived, the Villa's front door was locked and no one came to open it when I rang the doorbell. I went around back to the garden to see if you were walking the paths or sitting in the gazebo, but my heart was already pounding with the fear of finding, perhaps, that the windows facing the yard had been boarded up and not a single soul occupied the house anymore, because I had come too late. Still, I couldn't have even fathomed what I would actually see. There were young, handsome people gathered on the patio and music playing; no doubt everyone who had been expected was already accounted for. But you weren't among them. A young woman with short, chestnut-brown hair smiled at me from across the balustrade and lifted her champagne glass in greeting, but a curly-haired young man was already peeking hostilely over her shoulder to see what business I had there. He knew where to direct me when I mentioned you, although I realized immediately that as far as he was concerned, I had ruined the evening. And right at that moment it started to rain, even though the sky had been cloudlessly blue just a moment before, so they all had to move indoors and I waved to them, but no one noticed."

"What does that matter now," Laila said. "What matters is that you found me."

"That does matter," Brother agreed.

"Tell me about yourself," Laila said. "Tell me about Father and about everything that's important but that I don't know about."

Everything that's important. There was too much of it. He could have told Laila stories about their father and his artist-friends, and about how they could debate the night away on the subject of light and colors; or about the orphanage and the windowless trains that whizzed past outside. He could have told stories about fleeing and his nomadic years, or about the French Foreign Legion and the sand grinding between his teeth; or instead about the ships and the harbors—about the two weeks in Malacca, for example, which he had to survive without a single cent; or about how he had been a night watchman at a library in the Netherlands and read everything he came across by flashlight while lying on his belly on the floor between the massive shelves every night, and how he had committed as much as he could to memory. He could have told the story of his father's very last message, in which he asked him to locate his sister and, if necessary, to help her in times of peril—yes, he could have told her *that* story while omitting the main point, of course, for it wasn't the time yet.

He could have—indeed, all of that was important. Yet, he didn't.

"Let's talk about you, instead," he said.

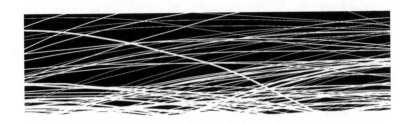

"I've never asked myself what someone else would do in my situation. For me, Monday has always been on Monday and Friday is on Fridays. From quite an early age, it was clear to me that cause and effect only have a connection if we ourselves put it there, and that whomever is punished is the one to blame. And so, I decided not to scream: the strength it takes for cursing the walls that I dash headfirst into time and again could help me to see through them instead—as if they weren't even there. I was sixteen and I'd been left for the first time, not counting when Father went away. I was colorless and frail like a flower that has grown in a dim room. If I quit asking, I realized, then people will entirely forget that I exist, except for when I happen to cross their path, and back then, I didn't know to be afraid of that kind of outcome."

"And you've never, ever thought that you should have had a different kind of fate?"

"Some people move through the world in such a way that their sense of order goes along with them. When they enter my room and see an open book lying face-down and crooked on the desk, they will, without fail, pick it up, bookmark the page with a strip of paper, and position it neatly on the corner of the desk, face-up, its spine evenly parallel to the edge. Those people must possess a great clarity, which keeps them connected to the overarching sense of order, and which comes to mind when they see the errors of the world. I don't have that. When I bump something in a strange room by accident, I always try to put it back exactly where it was before. I don't know whether the spot is right or wrong. I wish for nothing other than to be capable of slipping through the world without leaving a single trace behind."

"As if it were a mirror?"

"I was good at it in school. Everything they taught us was absurdly easy, but I realized before long that I mustn't let it show. As long as I'm a good enough student who causes no problems, I won't have any problems with them either; but if I'm too good, if I understand everything without needing their explanations and ask questions about things that they might not have noticed at all, I'll be penalized—then, in class, the teacher will call on me to give the correct answer in order to put down the others who haven't been able to come up with it; and at the end-of-year assembly, I'll be brought up in front of the whole school and their hateful glares as if to stand as a role model, but in reality, it's a pillory, and it'll be that way every time. As a result I was diligent, but dull. Things grew more complicated after graduation. I would gladly have given birth to a couple of rambunctious kids who weren't like me in any way, and gone around cleaning up after them, but the Villa didn't allow it—it was like a stone around my neck; our fates were intertwined and it was still there no matter how much I might have wanted to fade into the world."

"Because you yourself could be forgotten, but not your name?"

"I can't say I've come to terms with it. You don't come to terms with those kinds of things. Like how you can't get used to torture—you can only lose consciousness. Although it might appear

13

to be the exact opposite, it's actually always been very easy for me to make decisions. Decision-making means that something is being changed, doesn't it. *This* is the way it will be from now on, not anyhow else anymore. The chance for things to go otherwise has been erased. We've chosen our path. But there's nothing for me to choose. As a result, every decision of mine has been an agreement. I agree to what comes. No matter that it's hard and painful sometimes—that's how it is for everyone, inevitably, isn't it? I generally don't go out more than I really have to, just every once in a while in springtime—when the amusement park opens up on the river bend, I go and I wander around there; I watch the skilled sharpshooters winning stuffed teddy bears for their sweethearts and the flushed young mothers keeping watch over their sons galloping on the carousel horses. I'm not cheered by the fact that I'm not one of them, but I'm not saddened by it, either. And I don't feel like a spy there like I did at school dances, which I attended with the other girls just so that my absence wouldn't be noticed. One time on a whim, without really understanding what I was doing, I bought a ticket for the Ferris wheel and let it hoist me up above the town. And I just stared at the floor of the cabin."

"Do you know how many people never actually learn to be alone?"

"I've never talked about myself this way. At least I don't remember having done so."

Father.

"I remember almost nothing about him," Laila said. "Just that sometimes, when I was playing with my ball on the second floor despite being told not to—I might have been, say, two or three years old—and it rolled into his study, my heart would be pounding when I went in to fetch it and he didn't even look in my direction, so engrossed in his work; but even so—one time, he lifted his head and smiled, said something, but I was so startled that it might as well have been in a foreign language. Then he shooed me away. The fights started soon after. They always closed the doors so I wouldn't hear, and I didn't. He didn't leave his study door open anymore then, either. And so, I never did find out what on earth he was writing."

Mother.

"Father never talked about Mother with bitterness," Brother said, "because he saw himself as the guilty party. Although he did talk about her a lot. I knew about you the whole time, too; I knew I had a sister. Losing you really was the greatest punishment for Father; nothing could ease it, not even me. But Father always called her Mother, even though she herself hadn't carried me, you know; so I've never had another Mother. I don't want to see her picture. Let me have the picture that Father's stories painted for me."

Father.

"There were only a few random traces of him left at our place. His big desk wasn't removed from the study because it was too heavy for us, and every once in a while when I took some old volume from the shelf in the Villa's library, I would find thoughts jotted down in the margins in his handwriting. I read them without understanding anything, as if they were messages meant specifically for me; notices from the blank places in a photo album, just for me, not for anyone else."

Mother.

"Father would have someone from time to time, and I wasn't supposed to talk about Mother then. Some of them tried to find out from me what Mother had been like so they could be able to surprise him with only good things. They didn't *know* I lacked my own memories of her. They thought that when I didn't tell them, it was out of jealousy—that I wanted to keep it all to myself. They would've been right, but I didn't have anything."

Father.

"Red autumn leaves, leaving."

Mother.

"The first snow, so delicate that it vanishes when it touches the ground."

Father.

"And afterward," Brother said, "for as long as I can remember, he didn't write anything anymore. But he talked about the poems he'd left behind, talked about them a lot. He hoped that they'd be left to you. Maybe you'll find them some day. Maybe you'll understand."

Mother.

"She wasn't able to forgive him," Laila said. "She probably didn't even try. Everything had to disappear—everything. Papers went into the fireplace, clothes to the dump, she even smashed his big coffee mug on the kitchen floor. And the fireplace was lit for several days in a row, the flames dancing in angry, all-forgetting joy. That, I remember."

Father.

"That's true. He often said he would die in a fire, just unaware that he'd done so already. Then he tried to paint instead of writing, but he himself realized it was pointless. In reality, he wasn't good at anything; maybe not even at writing. Maybe he never even existed."

Mother.

"We loved the Villa, probably even more than each other. But while my love was mixed with awe—every door there opened up into a netherworld, from which I myself, in a mysterious and actually inexplicable way, had come—then Mother's love was split almost cleanly in half with rage. When we didn't have the servants anymore, she would still polish the floors just as frequently, still plaster every crack in the ceiling on her own right away, and would dust every last porcelain figurine in each and every room. Over and over. And she cooked a three-course lunch every day, an hour later on Sundays. It was a war."

Father.
"We couldn't settle down anywhere. He wasn't the one sucking life-juices from the earth, but rather the earth from him."

Mother.
"Everything had to stay the way it was before. That's what killed her in the end."

"Inevitably, at some point in every person's life comes the moment when he has to count up the promises he definitely intends to keep before he goes," Brother said. "For me, you've always been one of those."

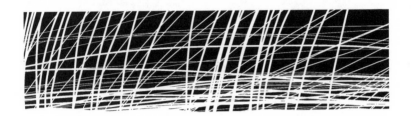

"At first, my hands would grow weak when I wound up holding some long-familiar item from the Villa. I wondered—how could I put a price tag on a clock that stood on the cupboard and measured my time when I was still a child? How can I set my parents' five-o'clock-teacups on a table in the shop window when all of the guests peering at them through the glass will still stay thirsty? But now, when I happen to come across an item stolen from my youth, I greet it like an old globetrotting friend who has decided to briefly look me up between his dusty travels to hear how I'm doing, too."

When he stopped by the antique store the next evening, Brother had a chance to gaze upon the Villa's silver spoons with his own eyes. Laila was pleased that he had been able to get some rest even on the narrow spare bed in the kitchen, since now, in the daylight, his cheeks no longer looked hollowed and the shadows under his eyes had disappeared.

"All people do here is flirt during the most lucrative opening hours; we're running a business here, by the way," grumbled the goateed antiquarian, dusting a heavy swan four times larger than life (that no one would ever buy, anyway). In fact, his claim was completely false, because other than during the town's annual fair, only ten or so people would stumble into the dark and somewhat musty shop each week, at best. Not counting the pharmacist, who would occasionally visit to play chess in the afternoons, and the wiser patients who knew to bring their prescriptions there on such occasions. They, however, never bought anything from the goateed antiquarian.

"You know, then maybe I'll take this painting," Brother said, pointing to a small depiction of a somewhat frightened curly-haired woman with a chubby baby sitting on her lap and holding, for some reason, a spindle in its one hand while expertly inspecting a large cross held in its other.

"That's pretty pricy, though," the goateed antiquarian said with a smile. "The work of an old master from the sixteenth century."

"Whoever sold it to you pulled a fast one," Brother said. "The painting's original is on display in Prado and is about two-and-a-half times larger. I always go to see it when I happen to be in the area. But I'd be glad to have something to remind me of those moments every morning when I wake up. What's more, it might be true that I once knew the man who painted that copy."

From his pocket he removed a roll of bills bound by a rubber band, and counted out onto the counter a stack that well exceeded the antiquarian's expectations. At that same moment, a large-weighted clock living its own secret life on the wall struck noon; a clock, which certainly ran when it was maintained, but the hands of which had been snapped off by time.

"This should be more than enough," Brother said. "Please have it brought to the Castle Hotel."

"Does that mean you won't be staying at my place anymore?" Laila asked in surprise.

"I plan on staying in town for a little longer now, and I don't want to be a bother," Brother said. "But I'll come by tonight if that's alright."

He nodded to the goateed antiquarian and walked out, his long coat fluttering behind him.

"That's just like my brother," Laila said, and blushed like a schoolgirl given a flower.

The notary was the first to stir. His letter, sealed in an almost starched snow-white envelope and marked with his large initials, was delivered to Brother while he was in his hotel room watching an old Western about a nameless gun-slinging hero, who had been hired by the men of a small town to defend it against robbers being released from prison. The hero had just been promised a free hand in the town to do as he pleased as compensation, and one of his first acts was to appoint the dwarf barber's assistant as both the new sheriff and mayor.

"I was asked to wait for a reply," the courier said at the door.

Brother had already seen the film once before and knew what happened next.

"Tell him I'm coming," he said.

"And so, you say," the notary continued, gracefully holding the ornate handle of a heavy teacup, through which his finger didn't fit, "that is, you *claim*, that the point of your visit is not to dispute your sister's rights to have acted exclusively as inheritor of your parents' estate, and naturally proceeding from that also not to appeal for the annulment of the amendments in ownership that transpired as a result of legal acts executed on the basis of mandates signed by your sister?"

"I already said that I came to visit her."

"Because—I hope that as a reasonable individual you understand me in this—if you ever should, by chance, happen to develop a similar intention, which wouldn't surprise me in the least, by the way, because it would be natural that you require the utmost clarity in these matters, meaning, if you should ever decide to undertake something along those lines, then I would simply like to tell you—not that I might be trying to somehow hint at anything, certainly not that—but I would simply like to say that firstly, you should, in that case, be prepared to prove any of your claims on the basis of significantly more documentation, you see, because as long as you're simply a brother who is simply visiting his sister, then it's, so to say, your personal matter—you *do* understand what I mean—but if you decide to be a brother who wants to dispute your sister's signature to certain documents, then the matter becomes, so to say, public—you *do* understand the difference, don't you—and that would in turn lead to a consequence, which indeed brings me to the second point that I'd like to make, for you see, you've only been in this town a few days, while I, on the other hand, have spent my whole life here, as a result of which I do believe that in some sense it might be prudent for me to advise you in this, you understand—to enlighten you about the circumstances, so to say."

"You invited me to tea. I came. Let's drink tea."

The notary's hands trembled slightly as he refilled both cups from the heavy teapot.

"What I'm trying to say is that several very esteemed persons in our town, I would say so much as the very pillars of our little community—you can probably imagine whom I'm talking about, can't you—in short, if things should, for some reason, go the route I mentioned before, if the circumstances should maybe change and you develop the desire to become involved in this issue, then several people could be, how should I put it now, *unpleasantly surprised*, which might not necessarily be the most favorable course of events, neither for your sister nor yourself, because, you see, there are particular rules in the capital and elsewhere around the world in general, but we have our own here, you do realize, and we've become accustomed to them, although you yourself might not be, nor should you, since I certainly understand that you've had more of a nomadic lifestyle, but on the other hand, your sister really hasn't, now, has she, and she also has the greater share of her life still ahead of her, so I can only hope that you will, by all means, give full consideration to any step you take beforehand. You do understand what I'm saying, don't you? Right? So, what do you say?"

"For us, things have gone the way they've gone. Now, we'll see how they go for you. Pass the sugar, please."

"Things are bad," the notary said, and lit a cigarette.

"Things are worse than bad," the lawyer said, waving to disperse the cloud of smoke. "Things are worse than worse than bad."

"Easy," the banker said. "First of all, we should find out more about him."

A rat-faced young man—the lawyer's assistant, whose name was Willem—came to empty the ashtray. He said nothing.

"We should figure out who he is," the banker continued.

"How, I wonder?" the lawyer asked.

The banker was a strong man who had already begun to watch his health and had managed to achieve enough in his lifetime to answer yes-or-no questions with a single word.

"We should play cards with him," he said.

Cloves always came on Thursdays, and Thursday it was.

He had already managed to empty the bottle of beer he was carrying with him, and had already managed to place the flower he had brought into a vase with water. He had already managed to go grocery shopping and to buy everything he always did. And while Laila made dinner, he had already managed to check and see whether the bathroom faucet was still leaking, and it was, and he had already managed to fix it, so that now it should definitely hold. He had already managed to read through both today's and yesterday's newspapers, and to listen to the radio a little on top of that. He had already managed to eat his favorite cabbage rolls, as many as he could stuff down, and this time was unusually somewhat astonished by why Laila had made so many of them. He had already managed to ask what news was to be heard, and without waiting for the reply, had also already managed to say how fantastic it was that at least one person—he, Cloves—hadn't left Laila alone to wilt in bleak solitude. This time, unusually, he had already managed to start to feel somewhat incredulous over why Laila hadn't already made the bed and gone to wash up.

Then, the sound of footsteps made by knee-high boots echoed from the stairway, and a knock sounded at the door.

"Good evening," Brother said.

"Hello," Laila said.

"Good evening," Cloves said.

They stared at each other until all was clear.

"It appears it's time for me to go," Cloves said, and stood.

How could he have known that once, long ago, the flower he brought would stand in the vase for the entire week, but then, little by little, it started to wilt already by Monday, then it barely lasted until the weekend, and now it was thrown out with the Friday-morning trash? Laila strove to remember what kind of a job the man even held. Director of the post office's delivery department? A clerk at the stationmaster's office? Bookkeeper for the brass band? She couldn't remember.

"I'll get going, then," Cloves said at the door, his flushed cheeks sagging, his spine slightly arched, and his gut hanging slightly over his waistband. Laila realized that she was seeing the man for the second time in her life today, as something obviously had to have impressed her the first time; but maybe then, long ago, each time before he looked at her, Cloves himself hadn't always known exactly what he saw.

"I don't understand," Brother said. "I don't understand how you've allowed the world to step on you like this."

"Because I hoped it would step over me," Laila replied.

"Even so."

"But did I really have a choice?" Laila asked. "I wanted, I really wanted to have a friend, too. But none of them saw me. Do you think that when they looked at me, they saw a scrawny girl with pale, thin lips and potato-colored locks, hiding her hands behind her back? No. They saw a tall, blue marble staircase; arching, golden thatched roofs; and a white stretch limousine parked outside—so what that it'd been a long while since anyone could drive anywhere in it. They saw my grandfather's surname and all of his ancestors since time immemorial peering over his shoulder. And when the mirage faded—and that happened as soon as they really heard anything I said—then they fled, helter-skelter; some didn't even say goodbye. You know, when that whole degrading process was over and they'd tricked me out of everything we once had, and I ended up here, penniless, unable to do anything about it and with only a bunch of memories breathing down my neck, then at first, I really wanted to scream and cry, but afterward, I realized that I was actually glad. Glad that it's all over now. That I'm free. That I'm myself. And that from then on, things would go both as well and badly for me as they might, but that it'd only be my own doing.

She gulped.

"It's hard for me even now," she continued, "when someone greets me out of habit, as if I'm still the way I was then. I don't know what to say to them in return, but they still do it—my old tutor Mrs. Salt or Mrs. Cymbal or the twin boys Hendrik and Hindrek—or, well, they're not quite boys anymore—whose mother used to be the Villa chef, or else Gabriel, you know—the bachelor photographer, with whom I was in love for a while in high school, against my will but all the more hopelessly. How can't they see that I'm not the one they knew?"

"I understand," Brother said.

"No, you don't," Laila sighed. "You still think that I'm just like you are. Strong. Someone who can handle anything."

"No," Brother replied. "What I think of you isn't something I don't see, because that's just the way I love you. But it seems like you've let yourself be bent the other direction. Maybe it's easier, but it's definitely not right, and blaming the world for it is even worse. You can stay hungry even while walking between tables heaped with delicacies if you never reach out your hand."

"I want nothing from them. Nothing at all."

"That's what I just said."

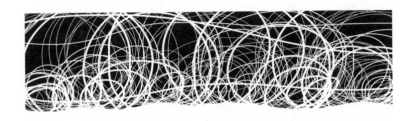

I bet it's a telegram, or else a catalogue big enough to not fit in the mailbox, sent from some department store, for example, the woman thought while rushing down the stairs—for who else would ring their doorbell at this hour? Passing by the kitchen, she glanced in and noticed a scrap of paper lying on the table—but she'd have time to deal with that later; as usual, her husband had left her a grocery list and instructions on what he'd like for dinner. Right now, she adjusted the folds of her bathrobe, brushed her hand through her somewhat messy hair, and opened the door.

Standing on the front steps was a complete stranger, muscular and tanned, far from unimpressive, wearing knee-high boots.

"I understand that you're in need of a gardener here," the man said.

"Yes, that's true—my husband and I have discussed fixing up the garden a couple of times," she said. "But we haven't settled on anything more specific than that," she added immediately. "We mow the front lawn here ourselves, but it's awfully overgrown out back, and there really is so much beautiful land there."

"That's exactly why I'm here," the man said. "May I come in?"

"Of course," she nodded, instantly forgetting everything her husband had instructed her about talking to strangers.

"I'm not interested in long-term employment," the man explained. "But if you'd like, I can restore the Villa's garden to its original state relatively quickly, so that if you employ someone to maintain it more permanently afterward, it'll be extremely easy for him to handle. Don't worry—I'm experienced. I've managed to get by at a number of countryside manors in England, and then we also fixed up a couple of hunting lodges near Wittenberg—although I worked together with locals there, since Germans don't trust foreigners all that much with those jobs. I learned quite a lot of new things from them, too, I might add."

"Very impressive. Perhaps you'd like some tea or coffee . . . or maybe something else?"

"A glass of water, if you'd be so kind. If I may, then I've got a piece of paper here—a contract—that I'd leave for you to look over. You'll certainly want to discuss it with your husband, too."

"Absolutely—we always make these kinds of decisions jointly."

"Just as I thought. And I presume he's the Villa's actual owner, is that correct?"

"No . . . in truth, the house and assets are in my name. My husband is an entrepreneur, and he thought it would be better that way; I don't really understand that much about it."

"Whatever is more convenient for you both," the man said, and smiled. "If I may, then I'll stop by tomorrow at the same time, we'll fill in the blanks, and I'll get to work."

"I'll expect you then."

The days when I also have some piece of unexpected news to tell my husband are so pleasantly uncommon.

She remembered it later that evening, when her husband returned home.

"You know, Mikk, an odd man came here offering to be our gardener."

"Great," Mikk said without lifting his eyes from the newspaper.

"So, today's that day again," Laila said and smiled when she entered the antique shop.

"That it is," the antiquarian replied, beaming. He had gone to the barber to have his goatee neatly trimmed; was wearing his best blue suit, a white shirt with a starched collar, and a black tie with a gold pin; and had even rummaged around to find his walking cane with a carved bone lion's head.

"I'd like to see the car that doesn't stop when I raise it to cross the street," he said, chuckling.

The store was fairly full: one young married couple—two endearing souls who hadn't lost anything significant in their lives yet. Laila realized at once that they could be shown even the store's most prized treasures, since they didn't have the money to buy anything, anyway. It was obvious that everything in the shop spoke to the woman. But when Laila started placing dollhouse furniture on the counter in front of her, she fell completely silent, almost motionless, as if she were utterly pooled into her eyes. Judging only by their youth, it was apparent that they couldn't have been married for very long yet, and therefore the husband didn't know his wife well enough to grasp what was happening. Nevertheless, Laila eased his impatience with a large portfolio containing old world maps, and removed the ribbon tied across a walnut chair to prevent people from sitting on it so that the man could inspect the papers at a table. The antiquarian would normally be cross with Laila for doing something like that, but not today—today was *that* day.

The antiquarian's son was visiting from the capital. On business, but even so.

"I won't return after lunch, in all likelihood," the antiquarian said. "Felix said he wants to talk to me about something, and it might take a while."

The long-faced man was silent.

"And that's your final position on the matter?" the notary asked. "If so, then we of course understand that we won't be able to convince you otherwise, but it'd be proper all the same if you'd at least attempt to somehow justify your decision."

"Especially since we've covered your travel expenses," the lawyer added.

The long-faced man stared at them at length.

"Fine, I'll explain," he spoke. "Over the years, I've developed my own reputation in certain circles, and I don't undertake anything that could cast doubt upon it. People don't play cards with me merely to win. They play in order to beat me. So that in the event that they should win, something amazing will happen. Something that'll be spoken of for years to come—something that might make a name for them. That is also the reason why I can certainly lose a few hands here and there—it's impossible to play the game otherwise—but I always leave the table as the winner. When you called me here, I presumed that you also understood it's never about how the cards fall. Those I play with have personally decided the game's outcome long before they sit down at the table. They've wrapped themselves up so tightly in the desire to beat me by any means possible that all I have to do is put a few links in place, and the chain that firmly binds them is complete. A few fall victim to their own recklessness, a few to their cautiousness, but everyone who challenges me gets the same end result; that's how I make a living. Earlier, you led me to a restaurant where he dines so that I could see him. I observed him from a distance for a while, as I always do with my opponents. If you've ever watched him with the gaze of a predator readying to pounce, then you'd have refrained from it likewise. Never before have I seen someone who so perfectly lacks any kind of resolve to win. I believe that if I'd proposed to him that we spend an evening at the card table, he would certainly have agreed, though only because he hardly declines a single opportunity that presents itself to him. Yet, the outcome would have been entirely unpredictable. It's possible that I would have managed to devastate him, but it's just as possible that he would destroy me. I watched how he eats: he forks food into his mouth in exactly identical sizes and amounts, but it was obvious that he is completely indifferent to how it tastes. That wasn't the only thing I saw, but it was the simplest. There is no way I can play him."

"Well, no great loss," the lawyer said, spreading his hands wide. "Simmermann's coming in on the afternoon train, perhaps we can strike a deal with him."

"If you ever need a player again and you're considering inviting me next to Simmermann, then don't waste your time," the long-faced man said, standing and putting on his hat. "Good day."

"Thank you," the banker said from the corner. "Actually, you've already done your job."

The long-faced man tipped his hat to him shortly, and left.

"So," the notary said, "what you win will belong to you, but what you lose, we'll cover ourselves. We'll additionally pay for your travel expenses, but there'll be no other compensation. I hope that these terms are acceptable."

"Not a problem," Simmermann said, smiling. "I'll sure milk him dry—don't worry, I've got quick little fingers."

"Then it's settled," the banker said.

"Maybe we should call it quits," Brother said when Simmermann placed the pack of cards on the table for a third time in order to go fetch more money.

"Why's that?"

"Because we both know that your little tricks aren't actually changing the course of the game. But you've started to repeat yourself, so it's getting progressively more boring. It's already late, too. And what's more, I don't especially need your money."

"If you say so, then fine," Simmermann said somewhat defeatedly.

"Sixteen thousand," the lawyer moaned, "sixteen thousand just gone up in smoke."

"In reality, he didn't *do* anything but merely prove what we'd already heard before," the notary agreed.

"Easy, now," said the banker. "Everything's been taken care of."

One streetlight had been smashed in the narrow alleyway behind the pub, and that's where they lay in wait. There were actually three of them, but only two shadows could be seen in the weak light emitted by the next streetlight about ten yards away; the third was standing concealed in a doorway ahead, as quietly as a mouse.

"Hold up there, brother," the heavyset goon who stepped out in front of him said. "Gotta lighten your wallet."

Brother's eyes flitted across the first man's bearded face, and then he peered over at the second—a somewhat shorter man stepping out of the shadows, whose straight hair was combed into bangs and who was wearing an elegant silk shirt, incongruous with his comrade's. He was snickering and rubbing something between his fingers, probably a knife.

"I got lucky at the card table today," Brother said. "I can surrender my winnings, no problem, but if you try to take what I brought from home, then I'll have to defend myself."

"What do you think?" the thinner man asked the stocky one.

"I recommend you consider the offer," Brother continued. "There's almost sixteen thousand here; it should be enough to last for quite a while."

"Let's take the money and be done with it," the thinner one proposed.

"You imbecile—then there'll be nothing left for us," the stocky one said. "We're taking everything."

"Can't say I didn't warn you," Brother said, and shrugged.

Viking, who was supposed to have attacked from behind, was the first to regain consciousness. The kick to the head had caught him by surprise and knocked him onto his back, so he hadn't witnessed the rest of the fight. He pushed himself to his feet with difficulty and heard Siskin groaning somewhere nearby—the boy's nose was busted and gushing blood. Cupboard was lying in the middle of a puddle, his face flat against the pavement and Siskin's blade embedded in his thigh. It took a great deal of effort, but he managed to drag them up to the wall. Siskin was forced to rip his shirt, which was already drenched in blood anyway, into strips for a bandage while Viking, who had maintained just a slightly more decent appearance, went and fetched a cheap bottle of rum from the pub. He poured some down Cupboard's throat, and it was only when his friend's Adam's apple began to bob evenly that he realized nothing all that bad had actually happened.

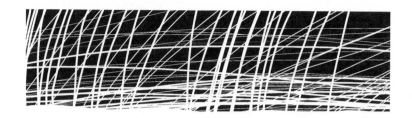

"And overall, Mikk," his wife said, "I think it's time for us to change the furniture in the house, too. At least in the living room."

"Why's that, Milla?" the man asked, setting the newspaper aside. "It's stylish. It's got history."

"But not our history," his wife countered. "What isn't your own is only nice for a short while. When I was little, we didn't have this kind of a sideboard or this kind of a chiffonier or a tea table with curved legs like this, or chairs with monograms stitched into the backs, and no one I knew had any of them, either, and I can bet that you didn't have anything like them at your home."

"No," her husband replied, "we didn't. But that doesn't mean . . ."

"I'd like to have something here that's truly ours," his wife continued, "I mean—truly. Even if the garden is redone to be the very same way it once was, then at least we're paying for it, so it'll be just like it's our very own, since it hasn't been the way it is right now for all that long, has it, and I want designer furniture in the rooms, from Milan, for example, and Oriental rugs, and in place of these strangers' paintings, I'd like something that I myself pick out."

"We've paid for these paintings and this furniture, so it's like they're our very own, too."

"Oh, Mikk, you do understand what I'm trying to say," his wife said, her voice turning syrupy. "Let's sell all of this, and let me look for something to replace it—something that smiles back at me, not glares. Why on Earth do you want to deny me that?"

"Did that oddball put that idea in your head, too?" the man asked, growing more and more irritated.

"No," the woman answered with unexpectedly biting self-assurance. "I came up with it entirely on my own."

"Two or three days, most likely; maybe a little more," the anti-quarian had said. He had been leaning against the heavy swan four times larger than life (that no one would ever buy, anyway), and although he really had every reason to be in good spirits, he still looked a little dour.

"Then everything's just fine," is what Laila replied. The impatient honking of Felix's horn sounded from outside.

"Yes," the antiquarian had said and sighed, "everything's fine. I've no doubt that you'll manage everything in the store just brilliantly meanwhile."

Laila had been tasked with minding the store alone for an entire day before, when the owner had been asked to go appraise old items in a nearby town, and naturally he couldn't turn down his son's invitation to come and visit—not after all those years. Genuinely, though, it had never been two or three days at a time. But the antiquarian was right. She would manage.

"You seem worried about something, even so," Laila had dared to ask.

"Oh, it's nothing," the antiquarian said dismissively, as if all problems could resolve themselves by saying it.

That had been morning; now, it was evening.

The truck drove up to the door about ten minutes before closing time, and Laila felt her heart sink when she saw what kind of a load it was bringing. The driver had been paid only for delivery, and not for hauling the cargo inside. The sky was heavy with clouds and a couple of drops fell onto the sideboard and the chiffonier and the tea table with curved legs, while Laila searched for any loose bills that might have accidentally slipped underneath the cash register. Offerings like that had helped before, on occasion.

"The rest'll be coming next week," the driver said. "Get ready."

Brother found her sitting in front of the store only later that evening; luckily it hadn't started to rain, after all. The ground level of the store was soon so packed that you couldn't squeeze through it anymore, and the heavy swan four times larger than life (that no one would ever buy anyway) was even more in the way than ever it had been. Some things needed to be carried up to the office, some things down to the cellar, some other things could simply be re-arranged. It would all take some thought.

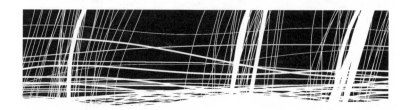

He stared. Approaching from the direction of the Villa, the clearing had suddenly erupted in front of him: after plodding a short distance down the dusky allée lined with tall oaks on either side, he inadvertently halted when everything around him was suddenly bathed in light. The back garden—bounded by a coppice and half overgrown with shrubbery, half with a thicket—rose immediately before him.

There was a lot of work to do here, in any case. One could only guess where the paths meandered and where water might have flowed in the garden's early days. The grass was taller in some places, shorter in others, thus leaving the lighter and heavier lines crisscrossing the space somewhat visible; although it would take some time to restore them to their actual form. All that was clear was that four wider paths traversing the copse began from the left edge of the garden, but nothing broke up the dense thicket growing on the right side.

He observed further. What was apparently a deeper and more linear ditch ran between the first two paths that started on the left-hand side, and a second, slightly narrower ditch had to be crossed to even reach the beginning of the path—however, the one closest to him immediately forked. Another line, maybe a footpath this time, connected the rear branch of the ditch with another set slightly downhill, so viewed as a whole, they formed something akin to a majestic letter M. Somewhere, sometime, he had seen something like that before.

He walked down the left-hand side of the hill and cut himself a path toward the first two of the four tracks. He became snarled up in the grass while jumping over the ditch and almost fell into the mud, but luckily only got his knees wet. Yet the path that now extended before him didn't actually lead anywhere—it was simply a long and likewise overgrown marshy track that extended just about as far into the thicket as the distance that now separated him from the Villa's allée. The remaining three paths also turned out to be identical marshy indentations in the overgrowth—the next one longer, the last two somewhat shorter.

The ground at the other end of the garden was less saturated. Only the rearmost straight ditch actually extended to the edge, but was already narrow enough there to be easily traversable.

Now, he had done a ring around the garden. Now, it dawned on him.

The garden was a hand, and the Villa stood at the tip of its thumb.

Over the course of the entire next day, Laila didn't touch a single
piece of furniture that had been brought there from the Villa,
even though she knew she should have. It was a new sensation
for her, as she had always felt pleasant around old things, and old
things had felt pleasant around her. But now, she was uncom-
fortable around them. She recoiled before them. They were like
former lovers who have had children with strangers meanwhile.
Their proximity was torturous. And because of that, she felt even
more awkward: they had still come back to her; they no longer
had anyone else. She should at least listen to what they had to say.
Maybe they were sick and broken and needed her help.

Then, in the morning, she pulled herself together. She wiped
down the tea table with the curved legs using a barely-moistened
rag and dusted the shelves of the sideboard one by one; she
brushed off the upholstery of the chairs with monograms stitched
into their backs, cleaned the attractive old paintings, and then set
herself to rubbing the chiffonier with furniture polish. It was that
last of these tasks that took the most time. The piece's drawers
and doors budged only with difficulty; it was obvious the chiffonier didn't want to share its contents with just anyone.

The reason why became clear somewhat later.

The chiffonier's large bottom drawer didn't want to open more than barely four inches or so. It seemed the previous owners had given up on the drawer, as Laila could glimpse balled-up packing paper and very old newspapers tucked away inside. Trying to open it by force did not yield results, so Laila cautiously slipped her hand in through the crack to see if something was perhaps causing the drawer to stick from inside. Something was. A metal bolt in an unexpected place had jiggled loose deeper inside and above the drawer. Laila had to remove all of the upper drawers piece by piece from the complex frame, and only then was she able to get her hands on the bolt. Now, the entire chiffonier was disassembled in front of her, naked like at a physical check-up, defenseless to her whims. A couple of brittle, dried leaves from an autumn long since past dropped to the floor from between two of the drawers.

Then she noticed it.

The bottommost drawer was a good six inches shorter than the others.

She flopped down onto the floor and reached her arm deep into the gaping opening in the chiffonier (barely reaching its rear wall), brushed the tips of her fingers back and forth across the unfinished plywood, and discovered that the rear wall was divided into two—that half of it was actually a door, which could be slid open over the other side.

That door wouldn't open easily, either. Laila had to fetch a flashlight to see whether she could find a grip for her fingers anywhere, and indeed there was a small opening cut into the upper left-hand side of the wood, but it demanded a great deal of strength all the same, and Laila didn't want to damage the chiffonier at all or use anything other than her own hands. Finally, the door gave way and revealed a nook, which contained a rounded, elongated object packed in white paper. Laila carefully worked it free of the space, closed the door to the hiding place again, and placed the package on a table. Before unrolling it, she stared at the item for a few moments and thought: *Just a short while ago, I didn't believe that I would ever still have days ahead that would divide my life into what has been and what is to come. But now, they're coming one after another, and it's not impossible that today is one of those days as well.*

The package contained fifty large, heavy gold coins with age-old writing inscribed on them. And a message slanting across wrinkled paper, greeting her with blindingly familiar handwriting: *"My little girl. I hope that you receive my gift when you know what to do with it."*

The handless clock on the wall struck, but it didn't hurt.

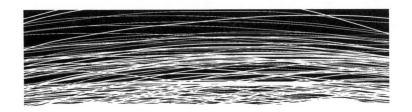

The consequences manifested before long. The notary had been the first to make his move, and therefore was also the first to take a blow. It was a trivial oversight, a mistake, the kind that happens every now and again: the sale of an apple orchard behind a dairy farm was drawn up incorrectly. The contract lacked the farm owner's sister's written consent. The sister didn't actually have anything against selling the land to a brewery, and what's more, she wasn't even expecting money from it—no matter that the orchard was legally a joint inheritance shared with her brother—and she would have gladly appeared at the notary's office to confirm her stance on the matter as well, but she hadn't been summoned. The entire affair could have been organized anew, but the farm owner had sold off all of his assets precisely in order to move closer to his wife's relatives in Australia; naturally, he had already received the money and relocated. No one knew where to find him. But as it turned out now, all he had left behind was a void piece of paper, and somehow, a certain group of mean and cankerous university students from the capital had gotten wind of the transaction—they didn't understand the least thing about local life and were adamantly opposed to the brewery ordering all of the apple trees razed and building its new production plant on the site. They could certainly drink beer, but brewing it wasn't allowed. The brewery was angered by this, of course (it had paid the money, in full), but couldn't do anything about the situation, and although they rationally understood that the notary was not to blame for anything more than a tiny instance of carelessness (if it even really was that—how was he to know that the dairy farmer's sister had her own say in the matter), there was nowhere else to find a scapegoat, and so they had to unleash their rage upon someone. A shiver rippled its way down the notary's spine. He could still keep the situation under control at the moment, somehow, but instinctively sensed that this was only the beginning.

The new balance of things found its way to the lawyer more slowly, and although the initial blow wasn't all that painful, he was subsequently that much more torn up from within. Barely five years earlier, the lawyer had divorced his wife, whose gloomy nature and husky build wouldn't allow her to transform into the kind of a companion required by her husband's rising position in society. On top of that, the woman's tendency to tipple on rum during long evenings at home alone was already leaving its mark on her features. Afterward, the lawyer started showing up at public functions in the company of a gorgeous creature with golden locks and the waistline of an ant, and who was—true—close to twenty years his junior, but obviously head over heels for him. Their wedding shaped into the nonpareil event of the season. The couple arrived at the church on horseback—the lawyer's dapple-gray stallion trotting a couple of paces ahead, whinnying impatiently, its rider wearing a snow-white tailcoat and a top-hat, grandly holding the reins taut, while the bride was atop a black horse with an old-fashioned women's side-saddle, so the edge of her long and silvery glinting dress dangled nearly to the ground. The lawyer wasn't ordinarily in the habit of making unreasonable expenses, but the next day, even the painters renovating his house woke up with headaches pounding in their temples (which they were only able to remedy with the aid of cheap beers), at the same time as the happy groom popped a bottle of champagne in the third-floor master bedroom, only for the couple to once again celebrate the start of their new life together. Up until now, everything had indeed gone well for him—he hadn't wanted children, and he was capable of handling everything else brilliantly. But now, his new wife decided to abandon her embroidery hobby (which irksomely strained the eyes) in favor of something that would keep her body in better shape (which was an admirable move in and of itself), and started taking tennis lessons. A couple of days after the notary was struck by the news of his own professional slip-up, the lawyer noticed that his wife wasn't wearing the large-diamond ring that he had given her as a present for their first anniversary, and which she had otherwise never taken off except for when going to bed in the evening. When the lawyer inquired about it with an emphatic tone of indifference, the woman suddenly began to stammer, turned pale, and trembled like an aspen leaf, explaining that the ring had started to pinch lately, and so she had taken it to a jeweler to be made a size bigger. This sounded credible in itself, since they ate well, but other details abruptly appeared suspicious to the lawyer: for example, that his wife sang in the shower at home after her tennis lessons, which she had never done before, or that she had been asking for a little more money for personal expenses lately. Even so, what could he say—prices were consistently rising, and even he himself had recently had to increase his legal office's fees. But he needed clarity. At the same time, it was a matter that he couldn't entrust to anyone else, because no matter how confidentially he might have tried to arrange it, rumors still couldn't be entirely ruled out, and right off the top of his head, he was unable to guess what might be more ruinous for his social position: a young wife's carnal ingratitude, or the public revelation of his own thrashing in a web of petty, unjustified suspicions. He had decided on several occasions to secretly follow his wife on her way to tennis practice, but as luck would have it, work obligations had always gotten in the way—major meetings of strategic importance, his personal attendance at which was by all means necessary. But even while sitting in his own conference room, it had become harder and harder for him to stay there mentally. He felt as if he was going crazy.

A week later, the banker invited both of them to dine in the club. One of his branch-office accountants had, as it turned out, borrowed a noteworthy sum from the bank without permission in order to invest it into a tempting but extremely risky venture in the hopes of rapidly doubling the money. It goes without saying that the man's dreams met with disaster, but instead of repenting, he somehow managed to disappear together with the day's till and a portfolio filled with documents, as a consequence of which the office had to be closed for the time being. Just like the notary, the banker realized immediately what was happening.

"It simply cannot continue on like this, gentlemen," he said. "We have to do something about it."

There exist dozens, if not to say hundreds of ways that a young woman can gain the attention of a young man. She can develop a cramp in her leg while swimming so that the young man has the chance to rescue her from death by drowning; her car could break down on the side of the road, so the young man can stop his own vehicle and see whether or not he might be able to help with anything. She can seemingly accidentally bump into the young man in a library while carrying a large stack of old volumes, and naturally the young man will help her gather up the fallen books; and on a snowy mountain slope, a broken ski can stop the young man whooshing past her. And so on.

But what can you do with a young man who doesn't laze around the beach by a swimming area or whip around country highways; who doesn't frequent libraries and isn't interested in competitive skiing? Now that's a question.

Dessa tended to prepare for things a long time beforehand, especially in the case of important matters. She had to know everything (or at least as much as possible) about the man, around whom her entire world would start to revolve over the coming weeks, because otherwise she wouldn't be able to decide what she herself was supposed to be like. Blonde or brunette? Or a redhead? Should her perfume be more carnal, almost brutal, or vice versa—a mere waft that brushes those who enter her space as she passes? Should her clothing verge on vulgarity, or rather display an exceptionally well-developed taste? And her eyes? Genuinely-naïve blue eyes ready to believe every vow, or proud green eyes, or enchantingly brown instead? Those who knew her would say on occasion (rarely, when they were asked) that they had already forgotten what she actually looked like, but the truth was even more dreadful—for a long while already, she hadn't had an appearance of her own at all; each and every one of her looks was a temporary adjustment to the man she was presently thinking of, and when she had finished with him, she allowed the look that had adhered to her to continue out of comfort until she needed a new one. But no matter. Her appearance was—albeit in a particular and unexpected way—the exact picture of what was inside of her.

She hadn't been to this town before, as the kind of people her customers hated enough to contact her usually lived in more complex places. She hadn't assessed the situation as being all that difficult when they had called her. Now, after making her observations for three days, she wasn't so certain of this anymore.

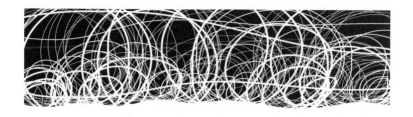

The lawyer's assistant—the rat-faced young man named Willem—loved order. Or, to be more precise: he was intolerant of disorder, and passionately so. Because although he saw it as his duty to enforce a clear and strict system everywhere that he had the opportunity for doing so (in the lawyer's record room, for example), we would be wrong to use words like "loved" or "hated" in his regard. For to Willem, they were meaningless. Likewise, by doing so, we would be crossing our names off of the list of those worthy of respect in his eyes. And that error would be inexcusable. We are even being a little risky by employing the word "passionate," but we'll luck out this time, all the same.

For about a week, rat-faced Willem had expected his boss to issue the order to execute procedures, the need for which was logical and self-evident based on the events that had transpired. When this order didn't come, Willem decided to set about it all on his own, although outside of working hours, since an investigation done in such a manner wouldn't be official, of course. Regardless—what was to happen in due course could not fail to occur, even though his boss (whose mind was preoccupied by the splitting of his tiny personal worries to an impermissible extent) didn't care about his own obligations sufficiently enough. There were still some untouched by the plight.

So, what did rat-faced Willem do? After work, he dined at Emma's Pancake House two blocks down from the office, just as he regularly did, but abstained from going to the Philatelists' Club. Instead, he made his way to the Vital Statistics Bureau and ordered a large number of thick, dust-covered volumes from the records department for viewing—several, because due to his lack of experience in private life, Willem wasn't very skilled at gauging people's age by eye. As there was no place for mistakes in his world, he moved only along definite tracks and wasn't concerned by the fact that it took more time that way. Even so, the first find took him longer than he had counted on. He had just managed to ascertain Laila's birthdate from a copy of her birth certificate when an official—a young woman with heavy glasses and long, dark hair worn in a ponytail—came to whisper into his ear that the archives would be closing in a few minutes, but he was welcome to come again the next day. Not a single other soul occupied the room apart from the two of them.

And the next day, he did return; although he arrived a little later than the first time, since he had taken his other suit to the cleaners on the way there. He began again from where he had left off before, and, poring over all of the documents carefully, determined over the course of the evening that the individual he was searching for couldn't be found within the five years preceding or following Laila's birth. That made him pause for a moment. It wasn't impossible that Laila's brother had been born in some other town; on their parents' summer vacation, for instance. But in spite of that, it should still be noted in the local resident registration, which was kept at the city government. Rat-faced Willem breathed a little more easily because, although he had a dentist appointment scheduled for the next day—which would otherwise have extended the time he'd need by a day, since the dentist's office was located at least a twenty-minute walk from the office and he definitely wouldn't have had enough time to get back to the archive before it closed—he would instead be able to reach the city government building, which was in the same direction.

Yet, the trip to the city government was a disappointment. After Laila's birth, no one else at all was registered at the Villa's address—not even any new servants had come to replace those who had left four years later.

He first noticed the woman while descending the stairs of the hotel that morning, and it couldn't have gone any other way, as the woman was there to be noticed. She had long, coal-black hair that spilled down across her shoulders; her eyes were slightly misty, like two poems; her skin was unblemished and creamy; and the dark red of her tight lips appeared to be their natural color. She had draped her light beige-colored suede jacket over the back of the chair, her golden-glinting silk blouse was loose and rested on her breasts in a way that one could just barely sense their curves, but indicated that she obviously shouldn't be ashamed of them. She was sitting with her legs crossed, her long Mediterranean-patterned skirt spilling loosely over her small, soft boots. She was sitting and waiting.

Brother cast a momentary glance at her, and exited through the front door.

It had turned stiflingly hot overnight, not a single cloud dotted the sky, and even the clock-tower bell echoed back fatigue and exhaustion.

The next time came a couple days later, and the woman was already entirely different in appearance then. Her hair was now a reddish-brown hue, and it bordered her tanned bronze cheeks in arcs that bobbed friskily. Her eyes, on this occasion, radiated a calm ability to understand her fellow man. Her fitted, high-collared blouse was tightly buttoned, but a tiny, almost perfectly round birthmark graced the left side of her lazy, pouting upper lip. She was sitting on a stool at the bar counter and reading, an espresso cup and an almost-empty glass of water in front of her. Sandals almost the same color as her bronze skin hung at the end of her long, straight legs. From a distance, it wasn't actually possible to discern that she was reading a particular Italian author's novella (which nevertheless required leisurely enjoyment) about a French silkworm merchant's travels to Japan at the end of the nineteenth century; however, that very same book was recognizably on Brother's nightstand—even though he had finished it long ago, he simply wanted it to be there, because the darkness meant more that way.

And yet, Brother said nothing this time, either.

Toward evening, he went out for a walk in the park just to pass the time, as he occasionally did. Truly, breaths came easier near the pond and the sounds of the park—the squeals of children playing, the chittering of birds, and a gentle rustling in the crowns of the taller trees made by an almost non-existent breeze—only caressed the silence he brought along with him.

The woman was already there. She was standing with her back toward him, her gaze drowned in the drops of water dancing in the air around the fountain. And she was waiting.

"Fine, then—let's talk," Brother said.

After a couple dozen words and steps, the woman hooked her arm through his like a lifelong acquaintance and, leaning slightly, would occasionally look up into his eyes like no one had ever looked at him before in all his years traveling, and after a short time, she laced her fingers through his. The woman's hand trembled lightly, as if she were doing so for the first time ever; her long fingers were strong and chilled like metal, and her knuckles tethered the man's hand to her own in a way that freeing it would have been painful. He allowed this all to happen, but not looking as if someone were just now showing him the edge of a secret hidden under the large gray tablemat of everyday life; a secret, the existence of which he had indeed long since suspected, but hadn't allowed himself to believe. They spoke at length, but about nothing of consequence. A sidelong observer could easily have been left with the impression that they were a man and woman who were on the verge of falling in love with each other, or who have already done so without realizing it. Even so, when he proposed at their parting that they have dinner together the following day, he did it simply not to appear impolite.

The notary's secretary accidentally knocked over an inkwell, which spilled across ten or so signed contracts awaiting archiving, and the layer's wife was complaining of chronic headaches every evening. The banker was still in a bind with his branch office: customers were closing their accounts there en masse, and in order to resolve the temporary liquidity problem, he had been forced to cash in shares in an investment fund that had been stable for a long period of time; shares, which launched into an unexpected rise two days later. However, all those kinds of things shouldn't have lasted for very much longer.

"And now?" the lawyer asked.

"We wait," the banker replied. "He's in good hands."

"We've employed . . ." the notary inquired.

"An artist," the banker said.

The banker was right. She truly was an artist, one of the greatest in her field.

Scores of homes wrecked, and in addition to the dozen or so who got off easily with suicide, a further countless number of cynical, burned-out human shells who were unable to believe in anything anymore, to be stimulated by anything, and who recoiled at every warm greeting, but nevertheless remembered her—Dessa, the only patch of sunshine in their dreary lives that followed.

There were no better hands.

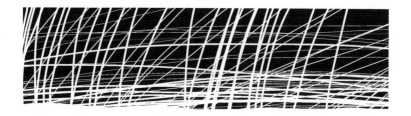

When rat-faced Willem had undertaken something, he wouldn't quit all that easily. Luckily, he had had to sit in the dentist's waiting room an extremely long time, which provided him an opportunity to consider the situation more thoroughly. In the case that Laila's parents had adhered to the norms of their union in the prescribed manner and the man was Laila's brother notwithstanding, the absence of a corresponding entry in the population registry could mean only one thing: for some unknown reason, Brother had not gone to live at the Villa with his parents. Yet based on that, one could deduce in turn that the man might not be Laila's full brother, and instead a half-brother born outside of wedlock and who was called a "brother" only in the interests of brevity, as people sometimes do. Proceeding from that, though, Willem could conclude that he must again review the birth registry for children born outside of wedlock, but it wouldn't be possible to do that today anymore due to the late hour.

As always, the dentist had nothing for him other than words of congratulations for his impeccably cared-for teeth, in which not a single cavity could be found.

The man was waiting for him behind the Villa, and had apparently been there for an hour or more already, since his entire attitude emanated impatience, even though he was forcing himself to remain calm with obvious effort. When Brother finally came, quite exhausted and sweaty from the day's work, he had no choice but to stop. He set his tools down.

"So, it's you, then," the man said.

"It's me," Brother nodded.

"Tell me, what do you want?" the man asked. "We purchased our house through an honest transaction, from a respectable person. It's our home now. We like it here."

"I've never doubted that," Brother said.

"What the hell are you sticking yourself into our lives for, then?!" the man demanded, becoming more and more irritated, but then startled and looked around to make sure no one had noticed them.

"Your wife hired me to fix up your garden," Brother said, shrugging. "I thought you knew."

"So, you take me for a fool, do you," the man said sulkily. "Don't you go thinking that I don't know why you're here."

"I told you."

"I know what happened to the notary who drew up our purchase agreement," the man continued, now almost at a whisper.

"And to the lawyer. And to the banker. You don't have to go trying to pull the wool over my eyes."

"Why should that have anything to do with me?" Brother asked incredulously. "Misfortunes can befall anyone."

"It does have to do with you," the man said, raising his voice, "because this morning, a ship that's carrying my cargo was arrested at the dock in Liverpool. That's never happened before, never! I've always had everything in order! And if that ship doesn't arrive here on time, then the fines'll be so large that they could wipe me out completely—do you understand?"

"I'm very sorry to hear that," Brother said, "but perhaps you might excuse me. I have another engagement ahead of me tonight . . ."

"Listen here," the man exclaimed, grabbing Brother by the shoulder. "When we bought this house, we truly didn't know. I give you my honest word! My wife probably doesn't know even now, although I was informed of it later. But what could we do about it anymore? We aren't the guilty parties! What do you want from us?"

"At the moment, only for you to let go of me," Brother said, trying to politely remove the man's grip.

"I swear—I've always done business honestly," the man sighed, releasing him.

"I believe you."

"And my ship . . ." the man groaned with so much distress that it was no longer a question or a plea.

"That must be some kind of a misunderstanding," Brother said, slinging his gardening tools over his shoulder. "Good day."

"I chose the dish according to who you are right now," Brother said, filling their glasses. "But I selected the wine according to how you were when I saw you in the hotel foyer for the first time."

The woman startled.

But maybe that's the key to him, she thought, regaining her composure immediately. *Being new every time. Maybe that's why he hasn't once called me by the name I told him?* Staring at her from inside a rolled lettuce leaf were three snow-white cubes of goat cheese, as well as a massive green olive crowning a mound of diced tomatoes with coriander and basil.

They were sitting along the ivy-covered back wall. Ell, who was serving the tables at the windows, was a distant relative of Laila's landlord, and was therefore well aware of her mysterious brother.

"He usually doesn't dress like that," she said, commenting on Brother's elegant dark suit, his pale-striped shirt, and gleaming-blue tie. "He usually puts on whatever is closest at hand."

Instead of his knee-high boots, Brother currently wore shoes made of pliable black leather, comfortable in spite of the fact that he was wearing them for the first time. But the woman was also worth the effort: her long mustard-yellow dress left her shoulders bare, while the heavy silk emphasized the flawless smoothness of her soft skin. As did the dense milky pearls around her neck.

"Even so, I don't like that girl," said Betty, at whose table they were seated.

"That's not a girl," said Jon the barman. "Have you never seen a girl before?"

The pair had bowls of creamy salmon soup set before them, the woman was saying something, the man listening without averting his gaze and wearing the faint hint of a smile.

"I don't know why I don't like her," Betty said. "I just don't. End of story."

"You're just jealous that you don't have that kind of a guy, what else," said Ell.

None of them saw how, while talking on and on, speaking in an almost hypnotizing monotone voice, the woman gingerly placed her long-fingered hand over the man's own. He allowed it to lie there for a few moments. Then, the man spread his fingers wide so that his thumb and pinkie emerged from beneath the woman's hand—one on the one side, the other on the other, then raised them up over the woman's hand in turn and held it in place, barely noticeably squeezing it. His middle three fingers slowly surfaced between the woman's, bending them ever so slightly.

Well, well, the woman thought, closing her eyes and inhaling long and audibly. *Now just a little flush in my cheeks, and we're in business.*

At the same time, the man had placed the tip of his middle finger on the knuckle of her own, and lifted up the rest of his hand. And he pushed—gently, using only a fraction of his strength, with a message that no one could fail to recognize, gently, decisively, as if he was afraid of breaking it, gently, intolerant of objection, slowly—her hand away.

Nothing showed outwardly, but it was like an electric shock; like a first kiss; like a sudden shooting pain in your tooth; like waking up with spotlights aimed at your face; like your favorite music turned up to an unbearable volume; like free-fall. Annihilatingly bright, thrillingly painful. She opened her eyes and saw everything anew.

"And here's the main course," the man said cheerfully, as if it surprised him. The waitress placed stuffed partridge before her, while Brother was served veal strips in Marsala sauce. Both had sides of fresh spinach.

"No one's ever wanted *that* before," Betty said appreciatively a short time later, returning with the dessert order.

Indeed—the restaurant was certainly good enough that people didn't dare to ask what the unfamiliar-named foods served to them comprised. They could hardly be aware that "*L'embrassade du papillon*" meant black plums simmered in ginger, honey, lime juice, and rum, and served with Portuguese vanilla pudding. In addition to that, the woman had ordered coffee *au lait* with brown sugar, and the man a straight Darjeeling tea. They drank the beverages in silence.

"If you walk barefoot on the seashore, right along the edge of the water," the man spoke while standing up, "then sometimes, the sand is dense and firm, and it's as if you're walking along a hardened path. "But occasionally, when you return the next day, you can sink straight up to your ankles in the exact same place. Isn't that right?"

"I don't know," said the woman.

"It has nothing to do with the water level, warmth, or the direction of the wind," the man said.

"I don't know," said the woman.

"I realize, naturally, that it's not the way it actually is," the man continued. "But in an ideal world, such things would depend only upon who you yourself are at that very moment."

They nodded a goodbye to Betty as they exited.

"Now that's a true gourmet," she complemented.

"That's not a gourmet," said Jon the barman. "Have you never seen a gourmet before?"

They left a hefty tip, in any case.

"My entire life," the woman said, "I've thought that we select for ourselves what we remember. But that's not how it is."

"Fine," the banker said. "What can you do. What do I owe you?"

"Forget it," Dessa said. "You don't have that much money."

Her art was now over, but as everything ends sometime, she wasn't really all that upset. And she knew that in reality, the world was now just a little more beautiful.

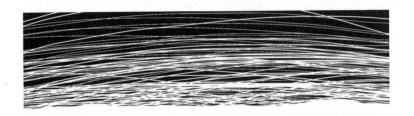

As the lawyer had set out a plethora of work assignments for rat-faced Willem to accomplish over the following days, which demanded extra hours at the expense of his own free time, it was initially impossible for him to continue his investigation. But after the bigger rush was over, he got down to it once more. Walking from Emma's Pancake House to the Vital Statistics Bureau, he went over his previous deductions mentally, and couldn't find a single weak link among them. The official with the long, dark ponytail and heavy glasses recognized him, and said a friendly hello. Over the course of the next four days, Willem made copies of the birth certificates of 39 boys whose fathers were registered as "unknown." When he had finished, a faintly discernable wrinkle appeared on Willem's otherwise perfectly smooth forehead. He hadn't believed that family values had begun to deteriorate in society at such a rapid rate. Disorder.

From there on, the process was not so much complicated as it was time-consuming. Before taking the next step, he needed to check the city population registry to see how the ensuing lives of all those young male citizens who came into the world without both parents had gone. For the first time ever, Willem had reason to regret having shown exemplary care for his teeth—it would have been exceptionally convenient to coordinate the large number of upcoming trips to the city government with dentist appointments.

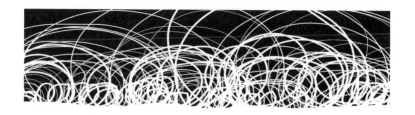

The goateed antiquarian could never concentrate when he was worried. Coming down from upstairs, he would forget already halfway what he had intended to do. Organizing papers at his desk, he would oftentimes stand up to pace back and forth across the room, and when he sat back down, he could no longer remember what he was supposed to have been thinking about. The numerical calculations he made in these moments naturally always had to be double-checked, as one mistake or another had certainly slipped its way in. And he would be simultaneously cold and short of breath, so after every short while, he would either open a window or close it again, and on occasion he would even get up wanting to open an open window or to close a closed one.

Cream cakes, Laila already knew when she heard the antiquarian up on the top floor that day. And so it was.

"Laila," the antiquarian called out, "could you be so kind as to pop out to the bakery across the street real quick? Three éclairs and two meringues should do it . . . no, you know what—get four of each."

Four meringues? It must be serious.

When Laila returned, the entire shop was already filled with the enticing scent of coffee. She flipped the Open/Closed sign hanging on the door so that no one would come and disturb them, and ascended the stairs. The antiquarian had set the coffee table with two plates and a large copper coffee kettle between them.

"How was it in town?" Laila asked, taking a seat.

"They're doing well," the antiquarian said, absentmindedly gnawing on an éclair. "Little Karl has started taking piano lessons."

"How nice," Laila said.

The antiquarian took his coffee with milk and a heap of sugar; Laila preferred hers bitingly black. It seemed as if everything really was in its right place.

"Felix thinks I should sell the shop," the antiquarian blurted out suddenly. "He wants me to move in with them in the city. I've accomplished enough already and can relax now, he says."

Laila didn't say anything in reply, only placed another meringue on her plate. She was well aware that the antiquarian wasn't actually partial to them.

"It'd be easy for me to sell, of course," the antiquarian continued glumly. "There've certainly been offers galore. But I know all too well what would happen then. They'd demolish the building and sell off all this clutter for nickels and dimes and build something plain and tall here in its place, open up a bar or a telephone store or a fast-food joint or something else temporary, and I'd have disappeared off the face of the Earth."

He bit angrily into an éclair and chewed for a while in silence.

"Why is that?" he asked then, obviously not expecting Laila to know. "Why do we read in the biographies of great men that their narrow-minded parents forced them to study law at university, while all the while they needed poetry and art? I myself wanted Felix to study art history, not law or economics, because I could've personally explained to him the basics you need for maintaining a business. But no."

70

"I suppose every person does have to be able to decide his fate on his own," Laila said softly.

"True," the antiquarian said, and nodded. "True."

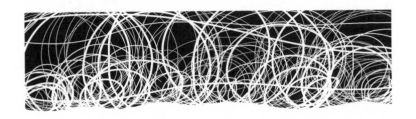

It took rat-faced Willem nearly two weeks to process the materials he had gathered with his characteristic meticulousness. It is, of course, relatively much simpler to find firm evidence for something that exists than for something that doesn't. He mentally classified all of the fatherless boys he came across into three groups: impossible, doubtful, and probable. Those, whose life's course was clearly traceable for a sufficient length of time ended up in the "impossible" stack. Out of the thirty-nine candidates, eleven had lived their entire lives in this town, and a further nine had left it relatively late in life—after graduating high school, in order to continue their college studies elsewhere. Although Willem did not rule out the possibility that Laila's brother could have become aware of the circumstances surrounding his birth only in adulthood, he was nevertheless convinced that news of the Villa's sale, which had stirred up quite a lot of gossip in the town, would still have reached him sooner if his mother had still been living here. Likewise, he didn't believe that anyone could completely purge themselves of their circle of acquaintances from their younger days. Out of the remaining nineteen males, he was only able to immediately eliminate one, for whom the city government had set aside a tiny pension when he ended up in a wheelchair after an automobile accident; still, he hadn't achieved enough clarity in the others' cases on his first go.

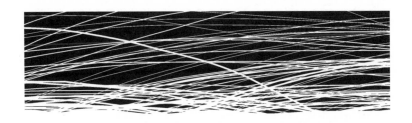

Brother had taken a seat for a moment on the Mount of Venus, and if he hadn't vowed one day long ago to start living better when he escaped with his life from an iceberg drifting off the coast of Norway, then he would have lit a pipe right now. The scorching sun was high in the sky, but he hadn't done all that much work yet today. When he saw the girl approaching from the direction of the Villa, he hopped back into the ditch and picked up the shovel again. The girl was wearing a plain dress and sandals that laced high up her legs. He remembered the girl and her short-cut chestnut-brown hair well.

"Hello," said the girl when she had reached him and taken a seat exactly where he had been sitting before. "I'm Dark," she added after a brief pause.

"Hello, Dark."

"That's just the way my name is, my parents gave it to me."

"That's how I understood it," he replied, wiping sweat from his forehead with the back of his hand.

Dark was silent for a moment, only watching him.

"I know you," she said after a short while. "You walked past the Villa's patio that day, when sunshine just as bright as it is now turned into a raging thunderstorm in a split second."

"And you were the first person here in this town to greet me,"

Brother said, and nodded. "You raised a glass of champagne in honor of my arrival."

"I didn't mean it that way."

"Of course," Brother said. "But you see, that's how it came across."

"I guess it did," Dark agreed.

"I suppose there are guests in the house again?" Brother inquired.

"The family's son is here, yes—they've organized a little party again."

"And you're with them, too?"

"Well, not exactly," Dark explained. "I perform for them. Otherwise, I teach music here at the school and do a few private lessons as well—piano and recorder. At first, the Villa's owners just didn't want their big white grand piano to be standing there collecting dust, so I initially tried to teach the lady of the house how to play a little, but she was completely hopeless; the boy would've even had talent, but he's got entirely different interests. In the end, he got so annoying that I quit giving him lessons, but when there are a lot of people here and I'm invited to come play, I always do."

"Ah," Brother said.

"Am I different now, in your opinion?" Dark asked a little teasingly. "Now that you know I'm not sullied by the opportunity to let time go pointlessly by."

"Time never goes by pointlessly," Brother answered. "Time piles up. We collect it in ourselves, no matter what kind of time it is."

"That's possible," Dark concurred, staring at her hand. "I definitely believe that everything that's been flows together with the blood in my veins, but if my heart is beating, then only the present moment is always ever at hand."

"Even when you spend a long time looking down into a valley from a high hilltop, or from a coastline cliff out to sea?" Brother asked.

"Especially then," Dark replied. "Only that in that case, the moment has no beginning or end. Nor do I myself, sometimes."

She said it just as casually as if she were giving a stranger directions, and she was.

It was already late in the evening, and the setting sun cast light through the narrow window of Dark's attic-floor apartment. They were lying side-by-side, their heads on a single pillow, their fingers interlaced, and the passionate flush hadn't yet sunk back into the ordinary features of Dark's face.

"As soon as I saw you," Dark said, "I knew that this was how it would go. At that very moment."

Brother said nothing.

"Don't misinterpret me," Dark continued. "And don't think that I just am this fast: no one in this town has known me like that. Even so, it's not what people call love at first sight, or what they use all kinds of other beautiful words to describe. I didn't even know if I liked you at all yet—I hadn't gotten a good look at you, in fact. It was more like a knowing that dawned on me the same moment you appeared before my eyes—your casual gait, your frozen look, and your sharp stare: that's how it'd go."

"I believe I understand what you mean," Brother said. "Really, I do."

"You're mocking me," she said. "You think I'm ridiculous."

"No," Brother said. "I don't."

"No doubt it's sort of like how it is for brides who only see their future husbands the day of the wedding," Dark said. "You know, in far-away lands."

"No doubt it is."

"I came to you like a lamb to slaughter. Or, no. Like a moth drawn to flame. Not unwillingly, but with a will that's completely conquered. Me, who always does only what I please, whenever I can. Why do you look like you've already heard all of this before?"

"I have," Brother said. "But I don't delight in it like I would have if you'd felt unrestrained."

Dark was silent for a while. They were still warm, in spite of everything.

"Does nothing restrain you, then?" Dark asked.

Now, it was Brother's turn to be silent.

"Not anymore," he said at last. "Of course, I've still got questions that I'm very capable of answering, but I don't want to. Is superhuman simultaneously inhuman? Is it right that we measure everything we believe in; that we measure it with an eternal, unchanging, and cold truth that none of us has ever known? Why is it that the more genuine and authentic the act, the greater the likelihood of regret? And so forth."

Dark stayed silent, since there had to be more.

"But still, there's been more," Brother continued. "There are things I've known all too well: what it means to wave goodbye to someone dear to you who doesn't even look back; or to run into a burning house to rescue your teddy bear—or your tiny son. For a very long time, I was gripped by memories, all kinds of memories, my own and others', real and imagined. They filled me up so completely that I no longer had room for my own anymore. And they were all painful—it felt as if everything beautiful and great had passed through me without leaving even the slightest trace, but I'd kept everything agonizing for myself; as if I'd watered my dark moments like a potted plant; had cared for them like bedridden patients until they'd started to command me, to order my every step, to inform me how I had to see. Until I shook myself loose of them. For instance: for many years, I wasn't able to walk with any composure down the streets of the town where my wife once fell ill; so unfortunately ill that it cost us the life of our unborn first child—up to a point, the splendid buildings there all felt like harbingers of death, and an accomplice to murder materialized in every one of its cheery inhabitants, in my eyes. But now . . . Now, those things have lost any kind of meaning to me.

"So, you have a family?" Dark asked.

"I did," Brother replied. "But what's there to say. I've been traveling without suitcases for a long time already, and mostly for the reason that I'd be left indifferent by what would become of them if I did have them; not that I don't appreciate comfort—on the contrary, I'm so comfortable that I'm unable to sacrifice anything for it; not a single second of calm or an unnecessary movement. The need to make good on promises I gave out of foolishness is the only thing that still holds me down at all, but since everything that I do in the name of those promises generally pleases me, I don't regret them all that much. You actually wouldn't want to know more, even if you asked."

"Probably not," Dark agreed. "Even so, you can't imagine how happy I am that we ended up meeting. You are staying in town for a little while longer, aren't you?"

Brother shrugged under the covers.

"Until what I came to do is done," he said.

"That garden? It really can't be true that you're only here for their garden, can it?"

"Of course not. I came to help my sister."

"And you brought me a present as well," Dark said, and kissed his cheek. "Thanks for that."

"Maybe," Brother said. "In any case, that's all I'm able to do. Because I've learned how to love others through trial and tribulation; but the ability to be loved has remained out of my reach, all the same."

"Why's that?" Dark asked.

"Love springs from the ability to prefer imperfection over perfection," Brother said. "From you understanding the shortcomings and flaws of your parents, your homeland, your children, and someone dear to you; naturally while wishing that those imperfections didn't exist, but still never replacing them with anyone or anything else, so what that those things might be flawless."

This time both of them were silent, until Dark started humming something to herself: a gentle but piercing melody that Brother had never heard before.

"Do you always sing?" Brother asked.

"No," Dark answered, laughing. "Only when you're truly with me."

"Then I'd like you to sing always," Brother said.

"Then everything's fine," Dark said, satisfied. "But I'm guessing you probably won't take me with you when you leave again."

"Darling Dark," Brother said with a creeping smile, "of course not, why do you even ask?"

"Thanks," Dark said.

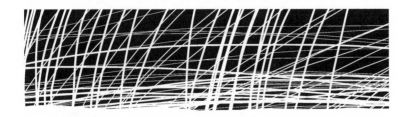

The bank branch-office accountant had apparently grabbed something else along with the day's till and a portfolio full of documents. Important data about the bank's security systems, for example. For how else could one account for the multiple inexplicable transactions made from the bank headquarters' most sensitive, most crucial accounts? Transactions that were done so cleanly that no one would have been capable of proving their illegitimacy in any way. Not taking into account the fact that according to the paper trail, either the banker himself or one of his deputies should have confirmed those transactions personally. Yet none of them had done so. They had been unsuccessful in tracking where the money had disappeared to.

His phone rang. It was the notary.

"Did you already hear what happened to the lawyer?"

"I did," the banker answered, nodding. "He personally asked me to help him keep the matter quiet."

After the lawyer's wife had informed them they needed separate bedrooms, the man—in the clutches of ever more grievous suspicions—decided to prove to himself in the town's tiny brothel that he did actually still possess all the vitality he needed. For a sufficient sum, a redheaded and plug-cheeked twenty-something moaned in his arms there in such a way that the lawyer was highly pleased with himself; but he had to relinquish an even heftier amount to the photographer who had been skulking by the brothel's back door seemingly by chance. Although he could be sure the affair wouldn't end up in the tabloids on this occasion, on top of everything else, the lawyer was now also beset by the gnawing doubt of whether or not his wife had found out about his little trip somehow, in spite of everything. Because a divorce filed because of his transgressions could ruin him financially—that, he knew.

"And how are you doing?" the banker asked.

"I'm doing well," the notary replied contently. "A couple of days ago, the antiquarian sold his shop with my help. He received fifty antique gold coins."

"Is that so?" the banker exclaimed.

"He sold it to that woman," the notary said.

A pause followed.

"And everything's alright with you now?" the banker asked.

"A telegram from Australia arrived this morning," the notary said. "The correct documentation of the apple-orchard sale is a matter of a week's time."

This time, the pause was slightly longer.

"So, we can no longer count on you," the banker finally stated. "Are you certain?"

"We'll see," the notary said cautiously. "I suppose we'll see how things go."

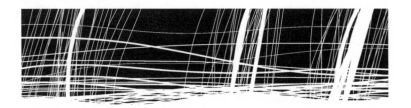

Rat-faced Willem was also able to rule out the remaining eighteen boys with unknown fathers relatively quickly. A full thirteen of them turned out to be all-around upstanding citizens, whose places of residence and fields of activity were not all that difficult to ascertain; another had possessed a dwelling until just recently, but was presently being detained in a pre-investigation correctional center in connection with a most serious case of tax fraud. Yet another required round-the-clock medical supervision as a result of his poor health and was therefore incapable of embarking on long trips, even though Willem was unsuccessful in finding the man's exact address. After some fair consideration, Willem also crossed off the name of a man who had graduated from military school with high marks and afterward earned captain stripes, but was currently on an international peacekeeping mission—his exact location was a classified state secret, but Willem nevertheless deemed the military credible enough to not doubt its data.

Only two possible young men were left over, and here, Willem arrived at a dead end.

Because the mothers of both were long since dead—one during childbirth, one as a result of gas poisoning when the boy had been barely two years old. Information on both children's fates was lacking. The town didn't have an orphanage where the parentless children could have been sent, so it was highly likely that they could have been dispatched to somewhere farther away—that is, if it hadn't been the case that relatives took them into their care.

Willem located both young mothers' passport photos in the population registry, and placed them side-by-side on the table. They seemed so different in every respect, and such was even the case with their surnames. Sea and Wood. Sea had dark locks and dimples on her cheeks; Wood had long, straight light hair, and was serious even when smiling. Which of them had been the one to whom Laila's father had been drawn with such an irresistible force that it had resulted in the birth of a child? Willem stared at the faces. Women like Sea left Willem himself feeling rather indifferent (just as he did them), since nothing was certain in their presence. But Laila's father, on the other hand, had been a sensitive birdbrain—he might have seen them in a different light. Could that sort of a bohemian personality have been at all tempting to Wood? Yes, if her plan hadn't in fact been to start a family, but instead just to get a child to be a companion in her lonely life. Wood definitely could have been that kind of a woman. Willem would have gladly envisioned someone like that close to himself, though not quite as a wife—rather, as a mother. His own mother had been an entirely different kind of person, and he generally preferred not to think about her.

It'll take an eternity to track both of them down, rat-faced Willem thought. *I've got to start with one or the other.*

Let's go with Wood, then.

He exited the archive and, still doubting his decision just a little, walked to an intersection with a newspaper stand on the corner. And then he did something that was simultaneously utterly illogical and, in its own unique way, exceedingly rational, and which pointed to Willem—against all odds—finding salvation before the story ended. Unlike many others. He walked up to the kiosk and purchased a pull-tab lottery ticket. *If I win anything*, he decided, *then I picked incorrectly. Because it'd be cosmically unjust for the same exact person to make two correct choices in a row by chance.*

He popped open the ticket, and not a single muscle twitched in his face. He had won—a new ticket. He threw the winning ticket in the trash and walked on.

The goateed antiquarian left his hometown by train. Felix had had important business to conduct in the city, he explained, and furthermore, all of his junk wouldn't fit into a single vehicle anyway. But Felix had made a firm promise to come and meet him at his destination. Brother had come to help transport his things to the station in town, and they did indeed have to take two trips. The taxi driver regarded Brother in disbelief, since the last time they had met, Brother had been wearing only a single backpack, but now he was loading the vehicle up to the bursting point with large crates. It was only when the first load had been entrusted to the stationmaster and they went back for the second that he grasped the situation.

"Going to the city, sir, are we?" he remarked crisply.

"What can you do," the goateed antiquarian sighed, and nodded not all that happily. "But my business will keep running," he added, peeking over at Laila. "Just a change in ownership."

"Even the name will stay the same," Laila added. She was wearing a white blouse closed at the neck with a brooch.

"So, something's changing and something's staying the same," the taxi driver remarked. "Just like always. Have a good trip."

It was a foggy evening, and when they had finally hauled all of the antiquarian's baggage through the tiny station café, through the waiting hall, past the baggage hold and the ticket counters, out onto the platform, and the train arrived, it was impossible to understand where the smokestack steam ended and the fog began.

"Well, what's more to say," the antiquarian said. "I hope that all goes well for you."

"Why shouldn't it," Laila said, and nodded.

It appeared as if the antiquarian wanted to say something else, but he didn't know how to put it exactly. He opened his mouth to begin several times, but only closed it again. Finally, he shrugged.

"Fine," he said, and took from his jacket pocket a large, heavy gold coin with old raised and worn lettering.

"I don't know how they found their way back to you," he said, casting a quick glance at Brother, "but I know from whom. Go ahead and keep this one, Laila. In memory of your father."

The antiquarian loved his son Felix more than anybody or anything else on this planet, but he was well aware that his son wasn't the foremost reason to feel proud of himself.

He sighed, boarded the train, and didn't look out the window again.

Brother and Laila entered the station from the platform and walked past the ticket counters and the baggage hold and through the waiting hall and through the tiny café, where there were four or five tired customers with wine glasses or coffee mugs before them.

One startled upon seeing the pair and raised his hand, as if wanting to stop time.

"Hold on," he said.

They only recognized Cloves by his voice.

There wasn't very much left of Cloves, but his hollowed expression saw deeper than it had before.

"I understand more now," Cloves said. "I understand with my head a lot of what should actually be seen with the heart; I even understand that it's wrong to be like this, but I'm incapable of anything else. Maybe I was capable, at one time, but that's left me. Though I remember feeling in childhood like the whole tangible surface between me and the world was made up of eyes—of hundreds of thousands of thirsty eyes that were ready to devour every flicker of reality—now, all of those eyes have closed like evening blossoms."

"I'm to blame," Cloves said, "for thinking it meant reaching adulthood. I thought that ideals are like toys you stow away in a cupboard when you grow up; or like luxury odds and ends that people who've never had to experience worry over everyday things can allow themselves. I was wrong. I thought that I'd learned my way to strength, but actually, I'd surrendered to weakness."

"It was always lousy of me to let my weakness be fed by someone who'd taken a much harder blow than I had," Cloves said. "Maybe by longing to be with you, I was just trying, without realizing, to build a bridge back to where I came from; but in reality, I only sealed your own path into a loop. It's futile to make the excuse that the loop trapped me as well. But it doesn't matter anymore—we're both free now. Is it better this way? I suppose so."

"I know that we shouldn't measure ourselves according to others," Cloves said. "I know: it's one thing to sacrifice the imaginary opportunities in your life in the name of someone or something; to make your decisions based on how it'd be better for those, who make your world possible. It's an entirely different thing, though, to put up with criticism from those same people; saying you haven't lived the way you'd have wanted, that you've given in too much and you don't deserve them when you're a man like that. But the strong don't thank anyone, so you can't have any other joy than the knowledge that they've become strong only thanks to you."

"Fine," Cloves said. "I won't take up any more of your time. The only other thing I'll say is that if I'd been stronger, then I might've even survived when the tribulations have broken me down to my basic particles. That some lofty aim could piece me together anew. Maybe even I'd have been a good brother then, too—to someone. But I haven't the strength for it, and so I'm trying to at least lose with dignity. And I'm not going to ask whether you might ever want me back, because I don't want your last memory of me to be ridiculous. If you're able to forgive me for the wrong I've done you, then you're going to do it someday anyhow, and if not, then there's no point in me asking you. Everything that might happen to me yet is of no importance. I'm like an athlete who's already broken through the tape at the finish line, but momentum will carry me forward a little while longer. Only that just like all of us, I'm alone on the track, because it isn't a race."

He fell silent, turned, and walked slowly out into the fog, where the train was picking up speed.

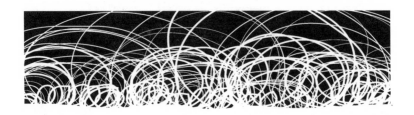

Not all that many people came to Cloves's funeral, although the brass band played and the stationmaster likewise came in person, wearing full parade costume to pay his last respects, and for some reason, all of the tiny town's three mailmen were also present. After a brief debate, Laila had decided to attend with her brother after all. The old-fashioned black dress with a high collar (the only suitable garment she could find in her closet) added a few years to her age and made her face look paler than she might have actually been.

Cloves had lived with his mother. She was a short and serious woman who had gotten by her entire life without anyone's help. Laila and Brother stood in the short line to express their condolences to her, but when they came up before her, the way she looked at them made Laila forget the words she had prepared.

"Don't say anything," Cloves's mother said. "I know."

Laila and Brother both bowed their heads simultaneously.

"Or, actually," Cloves's mother spoke up, stopping them from walking away by touching Laila gently on the shoulder. "Just tell me one thing, please: he didn't take more from you than he gave, did he?"

"No," Laila said. She would have said it regardless.

"Good," Cloves's mother said, and had it been another day, she doubtless would have smiled, too.

It was all simple: the coffin, the speeches, and the few tears. And it was even simple for Laila to toss her flower into Cloves's grave. She hadn't managed to say anything in the station café those few days earlier, so she did so now.

At the wake, there were more places set at the table than there were people who came from the cemetery, and Laila and her brother didn't want to stay longer than it took to raise a glass in memory of the deceased, either. Both were rather quiet that evening, although in reality, nothing could really have gone otherwise.

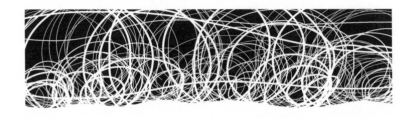

Most of his colleagues had acquired their nicknames by way of unusual features or some character trait, but the Surgeon truly had practiced medicine back when there was still a hospital in the little town. It hadn't been possible for him to embark for better days along with the other doctors, since his mother couldn't bear to leave her apple trees, and so, he had spent a while striving to keep his head above water by assisting scared young women in the back room of his house and by giving neighbors health-based advice in other cases for a small fee. Nevertheless, the apple trees ultimately had to go, since the Surgeon hadn't been able to properly heat their home (which really might have been unsuitably large for two people) in the winter, and in reality, the apples had never really been good for anything else than making a somewhat tart wine, which helped keep him from asking himself every night if his life might have taken a different course in some more far-off location, and whether he'd ever get over the damned chronic sneezing that had afflicted him ever since the hospital aromas disappeared from his life. For as long as his mother had maintained the strength to go outside, he would always walk with her back to that old orchard, though the house had long since been occupied by a large family with small children, who weren't bothered by the Surgeon and his mother taking a look around. But as one might expect, one day, his mother didn't go on that walk anymore; she didn't go anywhere. Luckily, it happened just a short time before the Surgeon, his sinuses clogged, made a mistake while operating on a rich man's girl, and so was sent to spend some time behind bars. He returned an entirely different person. But his knives were still just as sharp as before.

He was approached one evening as he stepped out of a café, which he had the habit of visiting for a few drinks of anise spirits in the afternoons so as to be relieved of his sneezing for a good hour or so. As if by chance, a dandy wearing tight-fitting checkered pants and a leather jacket stopped in front of the building—the type of person who always chooses the wine when visiting a restaurant in lesser-known company, but who never pays the bill. They quickly agreed upon a price as well as the size of the down-payment, and when the Surgeon had deposited the three packs of one-hundreds still wrapped in bank currency straps into his pocket, all that remained was for him to be shown whom the transaction concerned. To those ends, they met the next day in the park, near the fountains, and this time, the Surgeon had dressed in a clean, immaculately ironed shirt and a tie. The dandy looked just as he had the day before, so if anyone had happened to take a second, closer look at them, they would have marveled at two so different people being associated by anything at all.

"That's him," the dandy then said, pointing toward the park gates. "Bless you!" he added when the Surgeon sneezed. They nodded a goodbye, briefly, since at that moment, they both thought they would never meet again.

The Surgeon always knew exactly what he was doing, and was capable of carrying out everything necessary: unseen, he could track someone through alleyways packed with people just as well as on side-streets devoid of them—even someone making his way across a city without any apparent destination; he could observe from a distance, for days on end, persons of interest to him, just as well as he could stalk catlike across rooftops, noiselessly open a window, hold his breath for an outright unbearable length of time, and naturally also—after striking the carotid artery on his first slice—of pressing the opened straight-razor into the victim's own palm without letting himself be smudged with blood. Those kinds of deaths did not occur all that often in these parts, although frequently enough to arouse justified suspicions among the drowsy local police; nevertheless, the Surgeon had never left a trace behind, and on top of that, he never took care of people who would be mourned by anyone whose words carried greater weight.

Even now, everything could have gone the way it always did. But just at the very moment when, deep in the middle of the night, he leaned over the face of the man breathing evenly in the bed, the man's eyes opened as if he hadn't actually been asleep. He stared at the Surgeon for a few moments, then began to speak. He spoke softly, but rapidly, and it was almost impossible for the Surgeon to tear himself away from that voice.

"It's generally believed," Brother said, "that all types of sneezing are different, and therefore their treatment has to differ, too. There's hay fever, which you can treat by sticking needles into the right points in your auricle; and there's the common cold, which can be treated with an infusion of linden blossom and raspberry stalks. And then there's also nervous sneezing, which sometimes strikes those who aren't big fans of speaking in front of large auditoriums, and which can ordinarily be overcome by a sip of cognac; however, you have to personally believe it'll help. And there are others. Until all those little tricks have been tried out, people maintain the steadfast conviction that every form of

sneezing simply requires its own cure, and there's no point in trying to counter it with a single measure. I thought the same thing
until one time, I ended up stopping by an old kook's place near
Barcelona—a man who'd read Ramon Llull and the Kabbalah all
his life, and the dust from his books made me sneeze incessantly.
He taught me that in spite of everything, there also exists a tinc-
ture that eliminates the affliction at its roots so it'll never return,
and since ingesting it, I haven't sneezed again in the rest of my
life. He gave me a little bottle of it to take along and promised
that one day, it might save me or one of my loved ones from great
peril, but I haven't needed it in years. Yet two days ago, when you
started following me in the park for the first time, I remembered
it, and I fetched it from of my bag for you. And now, you're here.

"What the hell," the Surgeon said after considering it briefly.
"Let's give it a try."

When the innkeeper of the Lark Boarding House, which was
perched on the outskirts of town, went to collect rent about a week
later and found that one of her guests (who maintained a question-
able lifestyle but was always dressed fashionably) had slit his own
throat, the police officers initially didn't want to believe it was a
suicide, since although the dandy had frequently been in trouble
for gambling debts, they found in his closet, beneath a pair of
properly-folded checkered pants, an excessively large quantity of
cash for this to be true—three packs of one-hundreds still bound
in currency straps. On the other hand, it didn't seem at all credible that some unknown, villainous intruder had just gone and
left that unhidden fortune untouched. Somewhat hesitantly, the
young lieutenant heading up the investigation also tried searching
for the Surgeon, but heard that the man had put his apartment
up for sale a few days earlier and then left town, his destination

unknown. And since no one else was especially interested in the case, either, the police officers ultimately just gave up; they were long-since accustomed to living in a world where they were concerned only with what could be said out loud.

Rat-faced Willem now knew Brother's true name, but even so, he was very well aware of the fact that it was merely a tiny step forward along the path he had begun, and there was still a ways to go. For what good is a name if it isn't tied up in a network, connected to faces over the span of time, discovered in the trails that could demarcate the whole world? It was a mere word, a moment of moving air, a few lines on paper. It could most definitely be the case that the greater part of his work still lay ahead.

Over the first days of the new stage of his search, one disappointment after another befell Willem. He was unable to locate any of the Sea family's relatives, not even distant ones, and only one former neighbor had a hazy recollection of her; so hazy that not even his confirmation of Sea's relationship with Laila's father would likely have held up against a talented cross-examiner in court. But Willem didn't need that attestation anymore. What was worse was that after the birth of Sea's son, he had disappeared without a trace. Regardless, someone had to have taken him from the hospital, and someone had to have arranged Sea's funeral, as well. Willem had no choice but to infer that Laila's father had taken care of that, too, but inferences weren't enough for him.

Where had Laila's father taken his son? Had they rented an apartment here in this same town? Or did the man leave, an infant in his arms? So much time had passed that certainly neither hotel records nor ledgers of apartment tenants were still preserved—and even if they had been, it wouldn't have been any easier, since rat-faced Willem lacked a single address, a single lead to follow.

What might still remain from that time at all? *Does there exist something*, wondered rat-faced Willem, *that might allow me to peek over that high wall of time, if even for a moment, into tens of years ago when that tall, mysterious brother was screaming in diapers for his mother's breast, the taste of which he wasn't even destined to sample?*

And then he got it. The hour wasn't all that late, so he would still have time to get a thing or two done today.

"You're the first person to ask for them," the harsh-faced, long-necked woman in a purple dress had said to him. "The very first ever; at least as far as I know."

Rat-faced Willem was unsure of whether he should be cheered or embarrassed by this fact. He helped the woman brush the thick layer of dust off the hard cover, set it carefully on the table, and opened it to the middle. The evening newspapers published dozens of years ago had turned brittle over time and could tear at any movement, so he tried to proceed as carefully and slowly as he could manage.

On the front page of the edition printed on Brother's birthday was a lengthier interview with a hockey star from the area, who only commented in passing on rumors about his imminent marriage, and on the next page, a doctor explained the dangers associated with rapid weight-loss: after ending up in the bloodstream once again, toxins that were stored up in fat cells over the years can cause health complications and exert unusually strong pressure on the liver. The next day's leading story was dedicated to a water-main burst at a warehouse, while the reverse page spoke about a soon-to-open new history museum and the successful performance of the local brass band at a review held in the capital.

How different were the times, how different was the world, mused rat-faced Willem. *The people . . . but the people were still the very same, deep down inside.*

On the back page, he found a short piece about Sea's unfortunate death. Mourning her was her newborn baby boy. There wasn't a single word about where and with whom the baby boy was, only a reference to a generous admirer, in whose opinion the death was a tragedy that was completely worthy of public attention, as well as Sea's button-store co-workers' recollections of her kind and always-cheerful disposition. But that was obvious from the picture that accompanied the obituary, too.

Again, nothing.

Then, his gaze fell upon the adjacent article about a fellow citizen who had died while on a mountain hike in Croatia, and he realized that he had started his quest from the wrong end entirely.

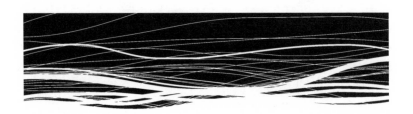

"You've been looking so good lately," Gloria said when Milla poured her tea.

"Why shouldn't I?" Milla asked with a smile. "Life has a completely different flavor."

A shipment of new furniture from Milan had arrived the day before, and Gloria was the first guest to whom Milla had offered a seat in their glossy black leather armchair. They were eating tiny marzipan cakes with very long-handled spoons, and both had also taken a small glass of excellent white port wine with their tea.

"But things aren't so bad for yourself, either," Milla said.

"Sure," Gloria snickered. "And when I finally get a divorce from that bastard, take a look at me then."

"What's holding you back?" Milla asked in surprise.

"Hah—he should get caught with something himself," Gloria explained. "I can't let him strip us of everything, now can I?"

"He's in pretty bad shape, isn't he," said Milla, who had last encountered the lawyer a few days earlier at an official lunch, to which she had had to accompany her husband.

"Maybe he'll up and die," Gloria said with a laugh. "I doubt it, though. Hatred only keeps men like him alive and kicking."

"I suppose you know best," Milla said, nodding. It was easy for her to say, since she had personally married out of love; at least that was how it had seemed to her.

"Hatred," Gloria said, apparently more to herself. "How's it even possible to live without hating?"

"Mikk is very angry on occasion, too," Milla remarked after a few moments. "Just a few weeks ago, for instance, a ship of his in Liverpool was detained for two days over some misunderstanding, and it was like he was at his wits' end. All he did was pace back and forth across the room like a caged lion and wouldn't say anything, but when he looked at you, then it was a look that could shatter glass."

Gloria wasn't listening to her at all, but instead staring out the window. Strolling down the oak allée toward the Villa was a man in knee-high boots, carrying a box of gardening tools.

"Is that him?" Gloria asked. Milla stood up to get a better view, although she knew very well who it was.

"That's him, yes," she said.

"Nice," Gloria said, nodding approvingly.

"Oh, he'll be finishing up the garden in a couple of days," Milla said. "And summer will be over soon, too."

"All too true," Gloria agreed.

"I've become so accustomed to him somehow," Milla said. "I can't even really imagine how it'll be when he's not coming or going."

"He's really that good, then, is he?" Gloria asked, smiling.

"What do you mean?" Milla asked, not catching on.

"Oh, come now," Gloria smirked. "It's entirely obvious that the garden is merely an excuse for you two."

Milla blushed lightly at her friend being able to think that of her, but said nothing so as not to dispel the thought.

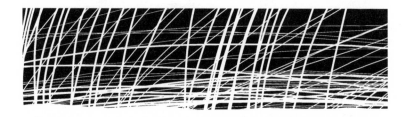

For starters, Laila decided, *I'll need to make a few small rearrangements.*

After she had determined that the store's commercial situation wasn't anything to complain about, she closed shop for a few days. The goateed antiquarian owned his own little cottage with a yard on the outskirts of town, which he intended to continue using as a summer home in the future, but he had slept in the store's second-floor office space (which had originally been designed as an apartment) quite frequently. Laila now had the rooms reconfigured into her personal living quarters, since she planned to never again wash a single stitch of laundry for anyone she didn't love. Understandably, though, the upper floor's present state—which the antiquarian had allowed to get out of hand long ago—didn't suit her, either. The task was readily undertaken by the young twins Hendrik and Hindrek, whose mother had once been the Villa's chef, and after the rooms had been transformed from dim chambers carrying the atmosphere of an old bachelor into a cozy and well-lit home, Laila also had her sideboard, her dresser, her chiffonier, her tea table with curved legs, and naturally the chairs with the monograms on their backs brought upstairs, and although she now had new mugs, she stirred sugar in them using the Villa's silver spoons.

So, here I am, then, she mused. *Still free, but grateful only for my memories.*

But that wasn't all. Now, in the ground-floor shop, she was able to undertake what she had dreamed of for years. An antique store doesn't necessarily have to be dark and a little musty itself, she decided, and so she rearranged items as she saw fit. Giving them breathing room, of course. And light, not just in the daytime: she plugged in all of the old ceiling- and desk lamps that were still in working order, so that they could glitter cheerfully in the evenings. She likewise removed the ribbons banning people from sitting on the walnut chairs.

And she had the dollhouse set up on a small table all on its own along the rear wall, together with all of the dollhouse furniture and tiny lamps arranged within it so that the lost world would return, too; and she placed a bold-lettered sign in front of the dollhouse reading: "Definitely not for sale".

How did she manage to do all of this? How was it possible for so much room to suddenly flood the narrow shop piled high with antiques? Perhaps because the first project that Laila had the twins Hendrik and Hindrek accomplish was to carry the heavy swan four times larger than life (that no one would ever buy, anyway) out of the store and onto the patch of grass in front.

"If it can't fly, then it can at least guard the building," she said.

Rat-faced Willem remembered clearly that Laila's father was dead (and Laila wouldn't have inherited the Villa any other way, of course), but he hadn't considered that fact to any greater extent before, nor had he rifled through the lawyer's documents. At the same time, it made sense that the little town's evening newspaper would publish obituaries even for those fellow citizens who had been struck down by death abroad. At least for those, whose fates could be of any kind of interest to readers—and the Villa's former majestically mannered owner was undoubtedly such a man. And if one were to infer that Brother had grown up (wherever) in his father's custody, then . . . then perhaps the solution wasn't so far off anymore, after all.

The next evening, Willem, armed with the correct date, was back at the library. Working there today was a different, older woman, stout and gray-haired, who didn't display the slightest shred of incredulity at Willem's request, even though an identically thick layer of dust covered that year's volume of evening papers, too. He found the article he sought in an edition published a couple of days after the right date, which was also natural, since back then, information didn't circulate as fast as it does today.

Rat-faced Willem read. He read about the fire in the hotel, read about the tiny boy who ran back to rescue his teddy bear, read about the father who rushed after his child and into the fire, from which neither of them escaped.

He smiled. Not, of course, because, but precisely in spite of the fact that it was a sad tale. He simply liked to know more than others.

When Laila descended the stairs in the morning to open up the revamped store for the first time, someone was already standing outside on the doorstep and peering in through the glass window.

"Welcome," Laila said, opening the door.

It was a man about sixty years of age or slightly older, but strong and with a healthy appearance. He was wearing shorts and a light jacket over a simple collared shirt, and was carrying a base-ball cap. And he was very tan.

"Hello, there," he said, "we'd like to ask . . ."

"Yes?" Laila asked, waiting when the man fell silent. Now, Laila noticed that there was someone else standing outside—a woman about the same age and just as tanned as the man, who was staring at the large swan four times larger than life (that no one would ever buy, anyway).

"That bird out there," the man continued, "is it for sale?"

"Of course," Laila said.

"Fantastic," the man said. "The thing is . . . well, we'd like to buy it."

"We'll pay whatever you ask," added the woman, who had now also entered the store.

"Come, now," the man said to her.

"We'll pay whatever you ask," the woman repeated. "And don't go thinking we're some kinds of kooks. It's just that we already have a similar swan, the very same size, out in our garden already, next to a little pond."

"Alone," the man specified.

"Exactly," the woman said. "You do know, don't you, that swans never change partners over the course of their entire lives?"

This is a cause for celebration, Laila reckoned. *I'll put together a little party,* she thought, and the thought didn't even seem strange to her at all. *I'll invite guests to come over and order food and cake from a restaurant and buy champagne from the store. I'll invite Hendrik and Hindrek and their mother and then I'll invite the teacher, Mr. Salt, and Mrs. Cymbal, and I'll invite the photographer Gabriel, too; so what that I haven't been in love with him for a long time already. And, of course, I'll invite my brother, thanks to whom this has all come true.*

She looked in the mirror, and the face in it recognized her again.

Rat-faced Willem had just finished his meal at Emma's Pancake House, but was in no rush to leave. Now that his search had reached its end, the evenings mostly felt empty and boring to him—pointless squares of paper instead of great treasures stared back out of his stamp albums; and even the task of sorting the lawyer's old ledgers no longer captivated him.

Suddenly, he sensed that someone at the next table was staring in his direction. He looked up, and so it was. He was being watched by the young woman with a long, dark ponytail and heavy glasses from the Vital Statistics Bureau.

"Excuse me," the young woman said shyly. "It's just that you haven't come to our office in quite a while."

"There's been no reason to come," Willem replied.

"So, you did find what you were looking for, then?" the chipper young woman asked.

"I did," Willem said, nodding.

"And what was it?"

"Oh, murky old things," Willem said with a shrug. "I just needed everything to match up."

"And now it does?"

"More or less," Willem said, because he didn't like to lie.

A moment of silence passed.

"Do you come here to eat often?" the young woman asked. "I haven't seen you here before."

"That's odd, actually," Willem replied, "since I come here every day."

"I come as often as I can, too," the young woman said, brightening up. "I really like the house-special pancakes with cranberry jam."

"Is that so?" Willem asked, raising his eyebrows. "I've never tried them before."

"You definitely should order them," the girl said. "They're simply exquisite."

"Some other time," Willem said. "I just ate my fill of ham-and-cheese pancakes."

"I see," the young woman said.

This time, the pause stretched a little longer.

"May I ask . . ." the girl began.

"Of course," Willem said to his own surprise, and nodded.

"You weren't planning on going to the cinema, by any chance?" the young woman inquired. "A really interesting film's being shown today, I mean. About zombies."

"It's the first I've heard of it," said Willem, who almost never went to the cinema, although at the moment, he couldn't have explained to himself why not.

"I'm very interested in zombies," the young woman detailed. "I mean, I have been for a long time."

"I know truly very little about them," Willem said. And then he hastily added: "Unfortunately."

"You know, we could go together, then," the young woman proposed. "I can explain all of the parts to you that you don't understand. To tell the truth, I've actually already seen the film twice."

"I'd be happy to," Willem said, and realized that he hadn't been in such total agreement with anything he had said for a long time.

They stood up, and everything was different.

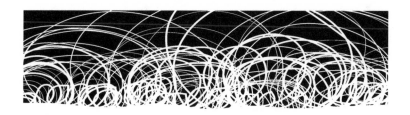

The woman began her story about the unbelievable scandal in such an ordinary tone of voice that it took a moment of tense silence before her words sunk in for the lawyer, and it took yet another for him to realize that what he had heard was ultimate and irreversible.

And then he suddenly realized why he still carried a lighter in his jacket pocket, which he customarily offered to women for lighting their cigarettes, as well as an unopened pack of smokes dried to a crackle for all of those twenty years since he quit. The smoke entered his lungs like a homeowner back from long travels, and a sweet exhaustion spread through his veins, dispelling the shock for a moment. But just for a moment.

Funny, the banker mused. *For me, things have gone the way they do for a man who merely wanted to see his friends off at the train station, but who accidentally got on board instead. This whole affair actually has nothing to do with me.*

That didn't mean he was unable to lose with honor.

For breakfast, he had toast with goose-liver pâté and a copious serving of caviar. *I'm going to miss this*, he thought, chuckling to himself. At the insistence of his attractive companion, he had also ordered a bottle of the hotel's best champagne, but only poured himself a glass for looks; more for the girl. In reality, he quite enjoyed how she alternated between squealing and purring by his side; he was even disappointed to be experiencing something like it for the very first time.

He had sent his family away to the seaside, so only the butler knew where to find them.

The banker got up late, around midday, said goodbye to his companion, paid the bills, and ordered his car be brought around out front. At work, he asked not to be disturbed with less-urgent matters, and had his secretary fetch the overview of his personal assets. It took about half an hour to draw up the documents and sign the money transfers. Then, he asked for a single espresso and drank it unhurriedly.

The phone rang. It had to be something important, since very few people knew the number for his direct line. But instead of answering the call, he removed from his personal safe something that every banker who puts his heart into his work must always have handy.

The pistol's cylinder held precisely one bullet. He had loved precision his entire life.

"Ah, you've arrived, ma'am," the hotel porter said with a smile sweet as honey when Laila entered. "He's in the restaurant, dining, and is doubtless already expecting you."

"Why's that?" Laila asked, confused.

"I assumed that you are coming to say goodbye," the porter said.

"Is he leaving, then?" Laila asked in astonishment.

"He's already paid the hotel bill, in any case," the porter said with a shrug. "Although, the maid did mention that his things are still fully unpacked."

But Laila had already breezed into the restaurant, where Brother was sitting alone at a table by the window, the daily special cut into equally-sized pieces on the plate in front of him, a small backpack on the chair next to him, and his long black coat hanging over the chair-back.

"So, it's true then," Laila said.

"Yes," Brother said.

"Why?" Laila asked.

"It's time," Brother answered.

"Will you come again?" Laila asked.

"If I happen into these parts," Brother nodded.

"Maybe you could wait until tomorrow," Laila said. "I've invited guests to come over this evening, and it would've been great."

"I'm quite confident that your guests will have a fine time, perhaps a finer one without me," Brother reckoned.

"Still," Laila pressed, not backing down, even though she knew that Brother was right. "Why so suddenly?"

"I simply have to," Brother said. "I promised."

"To whom?" Laila asked.

"To Father," Brother said. "Even after we no longer met, Father sent me messages, and in his very last one, he asked something of me for the very first time. He asked me to find my sister and, if necessary, to help her in times of peril."

"And then?" Laila asked, not understanding.

"Of course I promised—so what that it was mentally and to myself," Brother said. "I promised, although I knew nothing more about that sister than the few bits and pieces that Father had let slip about her. But even those were enough to be sure: there's not a doubt that she draws injustice to herself like bees to heather, and apart from me, there is no one who could come to her rescue when in great peril."

Gradually, against her will, the substance of Brother's words started to sink in for Laila.

"Forgive me," Brother continued, "but I must go. You see, it really is true that, inevitably, at some point in every person's life comes the moment when he has to count up the promises he intends to keep before he goes, and for me, you've always been one of those."

Now, Laila could say no more. She gazed at her brother in gratitude, she understood, she nodded, and her sadness was light.

"Keep your chin up," Brother said. "Perhaps for you, today is the last day that will divide your life into what was and what is to come."

He stood and picked up his coat and backpack so that what was to come could begin.

He strolled, a wide-brimmed hat on his head and his coat fluttering behind him; he strolled though the bright, sunny day with a slow tranquility, as if he paid the incredible weather no heed. Passing by a newspaper stand, he caught out of the corner of his eye the front page of the evening newspaper, on which a redheaded and plug-cheeked twenty-something promised to expose scandalous facts about a lawyer, whose name Brother didn't recognize. He strolled and didn't turn his head when a shot ringing out from the highest floor of the bank office sent pigeons into flight from the pavement, but on a narrow street on the edge of town, he did stop for a moment to cast a glance over his shoulder through a high attic-floor window, at which a girl with short-cut, chestnut-brown hair was humming a gentle but piercing melody, barely audible even to herself; a melody that he immediately recognized.

Acknowledgements

For those who didn't notice the bows made to Alessandro Baricco and Clint Eastwood hidden in the story, I point them out now.

Usually, nothing that I write is associated with any specific music. This story is an exception. Each of its three more significant female characters has her own melody. Here they are in order of appearance: Dessa is to the tune of T Bone Burnett's song "There Would Be Hell to Pay" off of the record *The True False Identity*, which speaks of her male doppelgänger: "When all the ladies / heard that he was dead / some wore black dresses / and some wore red." Laila is accompanied by Bulat Okudzhava sadly playing *"Nadezhdy malenkiy orkestrik"* on the guitar, and Dark's music is Chavela Vargas—actually all of it, but especially when she sings *"Yo soy como el chile verde, llorona, piquante, pero sabroso"* or *"Si vienes conmigo, es por amor."* And playing anywhere that no character paints the author's voice is Beth Gibbons singing "Lonely Carousel" on Rodrigo Leão's record *Cinema*: "The pleasures I seek / are far too discreet / for me."

While attending university in St. Petersburg, I socialized briefly with a man from the country of Georgia, who was studying painting and was in the habit of making copies of old masters' works for practice. He possessed a strange quality: no matter how unannounced a new person might end up visiting him at home (as it was for me, for instance), that individual's favorite painting was always hanging on his wall. In my case, it was Luis de Morales's *Madonna of the Yarnwinder*. The original is actually on display in the Hermitage, but there are also several halls full of Morales's similar works in Prado.

Rein Raud is the author of four books of poetry, six novels, and several collections of short fiction. He's also a scholar in Japanese studies and has translated several works of Japanese into Estonian. One of his short pieces appeared in *Best European Fiction 2015*.

A dam Cullen was born and educated in Minneapolis, Minnesota, but currently resides in Tallinn where he's translated dozens of plays, stories, and poems. He's also translated three published novels, including *Radio* by Tõnu Õnnepalu and *The Cavemen Chronicle* by Mihkel Mutt.

**OPEN
LETTER**

Inga Ābele (Latvia)
High Tide
Naja Marie Aidt (Denmark)
Rock, Paper, Scissors
Esther Allen et al. (ed.) (World)
*The Man Between: Michael Henry
Heim & a Life in Translation*
Svetislav Basara (Serbia)
The Cyclist Conspiracy
Sergio Chejfec (Argentina)
The Dark
My Two Worlds
The Planets
Eduardo Chirinos (Peru)
The Smoke of Distant Fires
Marguerite Duras (France)
Abahn Sabana David
L'Amour
The Sailor from Gibraltar
Mathias Énard (France)
Street of Thieves
Zone
Macedonio Fernández (Argentina)
The Museum of Eterna's Novel
Rubem Fonseca (Brazil)
The Taker & Other Stories
Juan Gelman (Argentina)
Dark Times Filled with Light
Georgi Gospodinov (Bulgaria)
The Physics of Sorrow
Arnon Grunberg (Netherlands)
Tirza
Hubert Haddad (France)
*Rochester Knockings:
A Novel of the Fox Sisters*
Gail Hareven (Israel)
Lies, First Person

Angel Igov (Bulgaria)
A Short Tale of Shame
Ilya Ilf & Evgeny Petrov (Russia)
The Golden Calf
Zachary Karabashliev (Bulgaria)
18% Gray
Jan Kjærstad (Norway)
The Conqueror
The Discoverer
Josefine Klougart (Denmark)
One of Us Is Sleeping
Carlos Labbé (Chile)
Loquela
Navidad & Matanza
Jakov Lind (Austria)
Ergo
Landscape in Concrete
Andreas Maier (Germany)
Klausen
Lucio Mariani (Italy)
Traces of Time
Amanda Michalopoulou (Greece)
Why I Killed My Best Friend
Valerie Miles (World)
*A Thousand Forests in One Acorn:
An Anthology of Spanish-
Language Fiction*
Quim Monzó (Catalonia)
Gasoline
Guadalajara
A Thousand Morons
Elsa Morante (Italy)
Aracoeli
Giulio Mozzi (Italy)
This Is the Garden
Andrés Neuman (Spain)
The Things We Don't Do

OPEN LETTER

Henrik Nordbrandt (Denmark)
When We Leave Each Other
Bragi Ólafsson (Iceland)
The Ambassador
The Pets
Kristín Ómarsdóttir (Iceland)
Children in Reindeer Woods
Diego Trelles Paz (ed.) (World)
The Future Is Not Ours
Ilja Leonard Pfeijffer (Netherlands)
Rupert: A Confession
Jerzy Pilch (Poland)
The Mighty Angel
My First Suicide
A Thousand Peaceful Cities
Mercè Rodoreda (Catalonia)
Death in Spring
The Selected Stories of Mercè Rodoreda
War, So Much War
Milen Ruskov (Bulgaria)
Thrown into Nature
Guillermo Saccomanno (Argentina)
Gesell Dome
Juan José Saer (Argentina)
The Clouds
La Grande
The One Before
Scars
The Sixty-Five Years of Washington
Olga Sedakova (Russia)
In Praise of Poetry
Mikhail Shishkin (Russia)
Maidenhair

Sölvi Björn Sigurðsson (Iceland)
The Last Days of My Mother
Andrzej Sosnowski (Poland)
Lodgings
Albena Stambolova (Bulgaria)
Everything Happens as It Does
Benjamin Stein (Germany)
The Canvas
Georgi Tenev (Bulgaria)
Party Headquarters
Dubravka Ugresic (Europe)
Europe in Sepia
Karaoke Culture
Nobody's Home
Ludvík Vaculík (Czech Republic)
The Guinea Pigs
Jorge Volpi (Mexico)
Season of Ash
Antoine Volodine (France)
Bardo or Not Bardo
Post-Exoticism in Ten Lessons, Lesson Eleven
Eliot Weinberger (ed.) (World)
Elsewhere
Ingrid Winterbach (South Africa)
The Book of Happenstance
The Elusive Moth
To Hell with Cronjé
Ror Wolf (Germany)
Two or Three Years Later
Words Without Borders (ed.) (World)
The Wall in My Head
Can Xue (China)
Vertical Motion
Alejandro Zambra (Chile)
The Private Lives of Trees